THRILLING TALES FROM THE FABULOUS WORLD OF HORSES!

Here are a dozen wonderful stories, including the adventures of:

- Ginger, who is determined to ride the unruly Black Boy . . .

- Stacy, who dreams of having a horse of her own . . .

- Jan, who tries to solve the riddle of Big Tex's strange and wild behavior . . .

- Lillias, who longs to succeed at her first horse show . . .

And many more exciting stories for everyone who loves horses.

More Horse Stories

Edited by
A.L. Furman

AN ARCHWAY PAPERBACK
Published by POCKET BOOKS • NEW YORK

An Archway Paperback published by
POCKET BOOKS, a Simon & Schuster division of
GULF & WESTERN CORPORATION
1230 Avenue of the Americas, New York, N.Y. 10020

Copyright © 1956 by A. L. Furman

Published by arrangement with Lantern Press, Inc.

ISBN: 0-671-43951-0

First Pocket Books printing May, 1966

15   14   13   12   11

Table of Contents

More Horse Stories

Crazy Over Horses

MARION HOLLAND

JANEY'S body sat in civics class, but her mind was far, far away. Automatically her eyes followed the teacher's chalk across the blackboard as he drew three large rectangles and labeled them: *Executive. Legislative. Judicial.*

But Janey was back in the middle of the summer —back in Westhope with her cousins. Again the gravel scrunched under her booted feet as she and her cousins ran down the long drive from the house to the stables. Again she saw Eddie, the stableboy, leading out the three shining horses, all saddled and ready for the early morning ride. Again she heard Golden Sun, the tall chestnut she had ridden all summer, whicker a soft welcome as he pushed his nose against her shoulder and watched with wise, dark eyes while she reached in her pocket for the bit of apple. She could still feel on the palm of her hand the velvet touch of his soft lips as he nuzzled the tidbit from her hand.

More clearly than the squeak of chalk on the

blackboard, Jane could hear the muffled thud of hoofs as the horses picked their way down the narrow path behind the stables, the hollow clup-clup as they crossed the little plank bridge over the stream. "It isn't fair," she thought passionately, "that only very rich people can afford to own horses." She would cheerfully have wiped every automobile from the face of the earth, if only that would bring back the wonderful time when people all had horses of their own.

The teacher's voice droned on and on, but Janey was conscious of it only as a persistent buzzing in the distance, like the large flies that bumbled noisily around the stables she was dreaming about.

". . . And finally, the Supreme Court, whose members are appointed by the President and confirmed by the Senate. Unlike the other judges we have mentioned, these nine men are not called by the title of Judge. They are called—who can tell the class?"

His questioning eye caught Janey's wide, intent gaze. "What do we call the members of the Supreme Court—Jane McGregor?"

"Horses," said Jane dreamily.

After school she paused at the door of the girls' locker room. She could hear the story being passed gleefully around by members of her civics class. Peggy's voice arose above the hubbub.

"Then she looked him right in the eye, and said, 'Horses!' Imagine!"

There were delighted and incredulous shrieks. Jane made her way unobserved to her locker.

2

"Oh, well," said Carol, in an indulgent tone, "you know Janey. She's crazy about horses."

"Crazy is right," whooped Peggy. "Hoof-and-mouth disease, I call it. Honestly, gals, I'll bet she sleeps standing up and eats out of a nose bag. Every time she opens her mouth I expect to hear her shinny—or whatever it is that horses do! First thing you know, she'll be *looking* like a horse!"

Jane slammed her locker shut and stalked to the door. "I'd rather look like a horse than like some people I know," she said.

Carol would have walked home with her, but Jane brushed by and strode on alone, kicking at the bright leaves on the sidewalk. It was bad enough, she thought resentfully, not to be able to ride all winter long, or even to see any horses except the junkman's poor rickety animal. But she couldn't even talk about horses to any of her friends; either they thought she was bragging about her rich relatives, or they just didn't listen. Except Carol, good old Carol. And even she had finally said plaintively, "Look, let's not talk about horses any more. I'm scared of horses, sort of."

"Oh, *no*," Jane had cried. "Nobody could be scared of horses!"

"*I* could," Carol had replied with feeling. "I was on a horse once—a horse about a mile high! The ground was so far away I could hardly see it, and my teeth were chattering so loud the old horse turned his head around to see what all the noise was. Then he opened his mouth about a yard and a half—you never saw so many teeth in your

3

life! I couldn't decide whether he was laughing at me, or just getting ready to chew my leg off, so I sat there and hollered, 'Get me down off of here, somebody!' "

At home it was just as bad. Her father, she knew, was proud of her horsemanship. She had heard him bragging to his friends about it: "Jane's cousins have been riding all their lives—practically jumped from the cradle into the saddle, but Jane is just about as good on horseback!" But even he hadn't the vaguest idea how she felt about horses. To him, riding was just another athletic skill, like playing tennis, and a good horse was no better than a good tennis racket. When she asked for a horse for her birthday, he threw up his hands.

"It's impossible!" he exclaimed. "Why, do you have any idea what it costs your uncle to keep up that stable? Even aside from the price of a good saddle horse, it would be out of the question for us to keep one."

"Good heavens!" her mother cried in alarm. "I should say so! Oh, dear, I do think a horse is so —so . . ."

"So what?" demanded Jane.

"So *large*, dear."

"Well, then, if I can't have a horse for my birthday, I don't want anything."

"But of course you'll have a party, dear. Why, you've always had a party, and it's always been *such* fun, hasn't it?"

"I don't want any old party," replied Jane sulkily. "All I want is a horse."

4

"And you'll need a new dress," her mother went on brightly, just as if Jane hadn't spoken. "I saw the loveliest dress last week, in Higger's window, I think it was. Just your type. It was rather expensive, but as long as it will do for the Fall Dance, too . . ."

"The Fall Dance?" Jane echoed blankly.

"Why certainly. You're going, aren't you? I thought you said Chuck Ryan had asked you."

"Oh, he *asked* me, all right," mumbled Jane. "But I don't know. Honestly, Mother, Chuck Ryan is an awful dope. Do you know what he said the other day? He said, 'Horses! Why I thought the horse was extinct, like the dodo!' Anyway, I don't want to go to the old Fall Dance."

"*Really,* Jane . . ." began her mother, in exasperation, but Jane had fled to the sanctuary of her own room where she could be alone.

At school she continued to dream her way through classes, doodling little sketches of horses on the margins of her notebooks. One day, in geometry, a piece of paper with a horse sketched on it slipped from her desk to the floor. She reached for it quickly, but not quickly enough. The boy across the aisle picked it up, glanced at it casually.

"Too short in the pastern," he commented.

With scarlet cheeks, Jane snatched the drawing. Short in the pastern, indeed! Well, maybe it was, at that. At least he hadn't said thick in the ankles, as Chuck Ryan certainly would have. She glanced sidewise at him.

His name was Grant Davidson, and that was all

5

she knew about him. He was new in school this year. He was tall and gangling, and she had often stumbled over his big feet in the aisle on her way to her seat. But he must know something about horses. She promptly resolved to get acquainted with him.

This turned out to be harder than she had anticipated. Every time she ran into him around school, she gave him a smile and a cordial greeting, and every time he replied, without enthusiasm, "Hiya." If only she could catch him outside of school and start a conversation—but she never saw him outside of school. He wasn't in the noisy crowd that descended on the corner drugstore at three-thirty. He wasn't out for football, she discovered by hanging around one afternoon and watching the squad practice. Of course Chuck, the big oaf, thought she had come to watch him, but that couldn't be helped. She finally came to the conclusion that Grant must have some kind of a regular job after school. She asked a few cautious questions of people, but nobody seemed to know Grant Davidson.

One morning, about a week before her birthday, she ran into Chuck at the corner, and they bicycled to school together.

"Well, today's the big day!" he exclaimed. Jane looked blank. "Say—don't you know what day this is?" he demanded.

"Why, Friday—isn't it?"

" 'Friday,' she says. Listen, dimwit, we play our first game this afternoon, and the coach is starting me at right half. How do you like *that?*"

Suddenly Jane remembered the dogged way Chuck had worked to make the team for three years.

"Oh, how swell!" she exclaimed warmly. "I'm so glad—and you can just bet I'll be out there this afternoon rooting for you!"

"Atta girl," he replied heartily. "Say, this is just like old times, isn't it? I knew you were all right, all the time, Janey. That's what I kept telling the gang—Janey's off the beam, but it's strictly temporary. A regular gal, like Jane McGregor, I kept saying—it stands to reason she isn't going to go on mooning forever about something as sissy as riding around on a horse, in a pair of fancy pants! I knew you'd snap out of it." Jane's eyes began to flash dangerously, but Chuck blundered happily on. "Stick around after the game, huh? We'll go someplace. And remember that date for the Fall Dance."

Jane exploded. "Chuck Ryan, don't you ever dare speak to me again as long as you live! Riding horseback isn't sissy—it takes a lot more brains and nerve and skill than kicking a silly old football around and rolling in the mud! I'd rather go riding any day than watch any old football game that was ever played! In fact, I'm not even going to the game this afternoon, so there. And you can just get yourself another date for the Fall Dance."

Chuck's mouth sagged open. "But you said . . ."

"I did not!" she snapped. "Anyway, I've got another date—I'm going with Grant Davidson!"

As she pedaled on alone toward school, Jane wondered, "Now what in the world made me say *that?* I can't even get a civil hello out of the guy —fat chance I have of getting an invitation to the Fall Dance!"

Well, one thing—she wasn't going out to the field and watch Chuck Ryan cover himself with glory. The big gorilla. Right after her last class, she dashed to the bicycle rack, grabbed her bike, and started for home. She took the first corner at breakneck speed, and nearly collided with another bike. The rider was Grant Davidson.

"Hi!" she greeted him, when she had recovered her breath. "Say, do you go home this way, too? It's funny we never ran into each other before, isn't it?"

"Yes," he replied, and rode on in silence.

"Oh, dear," she thought, "this is where I ought to start a perfectly fascinating conversation or something." But he was riding so rapidly that it took all her breath just to keep up with him. Soon they were speeding along a street heading for the edge of town.

"Do you live this far out?" asked Grant finally.

"Well, no. But I'm going this way today," she said casually. "And that's no lie," she thought.

The houses got farther and farther apart, the sidewalks disappeared, fields of ragged goldenrod bordered the road. And still Grant pedaled along in stony silence, and Jane racked her brains for something to say.

Suddenly he slowed down and stopped at a narrow dirt lane. "Well, so long," he said abruptly, and before Jane could open her mouth, he turned off into the lane and disappeared in a cloud of dust.

"Boy! What a brush-off," she muttered, staring after him.

Well, it didn't take a brick house to fall on *her*. But as she wheeled her bike around, she heard a sound she hadn't heard since she left Westhope —the eager nicker of a horse who sees a friend approaching. She wouldn't—she couldn't—go back to town until she had at least seen the horse, even if it was only a farm animal.

She thrust her bike under some bushes and started cautiously up the lane on foot. At the first bend she stopped. There was a farmhouse, old and comfortably ugly with wide, sagging porches, and beyond it a barn, a stable, and scattered out-buildings. A rail fence surrounded a broad expanse of sloping meadow. Grant Davidson stood at the fence with his back toward her, rubbing the ears of a bay horse—a little fellow, hardly more than a colt —who was playfully nipping his shoulder. In the meadow two other horses were grazing, a gray and a black. One glance told Jane that these were no farm animals. They were fine saddle horses—beauties, all of them.

Grant turned and went into the barn, and the little bay, with a toss of its head and a flourish of his heels, cantered off to join the other horses. If only she had an apple or a carrot, she might coax one of them over to the fence.

"I suppose I'm trespassing, or something," she

9

thought, "but I don't see how they can do anything more than throw me out!"

At the corner of the barn, she ran smack into Grant. He was wearing heavy boots and carrying a rake and a shovel.

"Oh—hello," she said lamely. So this was his after-school job. "Do you suppose they'd mind if I just went and talked to the horses?"

"Who?" he asked.

"Why, they . . ." she nodded toward the house. "The people that own them."

"Oh—I dunno," he answered evasively. "Horses don't much like being squealed at and pawed over." He turned his back on her and walked off toward the stable.

Jane stared after him, seething. "Why—why . . ." she sputtered. What did he take her for, anyway? Maybe he thought that if he was rude enough, she would get mad and go away. "Well, I just won't," she thought grimly, "at least, not until someone comes out of the house and orders me away." She perched on the fence and watched Grant clean one of the box stalls, raking out the old straw and litter. It reminded her pleasantly of the way she had hung around the stables at Westhope, watching Eddie putter around with his chores, but Eddie treated her like a human being.

She tried again. "Do you work here every day?"

He nodded without looking up.

"Do they—do they ever let you ride any of the horses?"

A smile flitted across his face. Then he replied

10

shortly, "Yeah. It's part of my job. The horses need exercise—more than they get."

Jane's words tumbled out. "Oh—do you think —I wonder—I mean, would they ever let me ride? I'd give anything to . . ."

"These aren't livery stable hacks," he replied scornfully. "They're fine horses, with sensitive mouths."

"But I can ride. Honestly, I can . . ." But Grant had disappeared. He returned in a minute with a load of clean straw and began spreading it evenly across the floor of the stall. Jane was almost crying with anger and disappointment. "I can too ride," she repeated.

"That's what a lot of people think," he said rudely, and went on. "You know anything about horses? Ever clean out a stall? Can you saddle a horse? Rub it down properly?"

"No," she said crossly. "The stableman did all that."

"That's what I thought," he replied, and continued his work.

The horses were grazing on the far side of the meadow, and Jane knew there wasn't a chance of coaxing one over to the fence. "Maybe I can get acquainted with the people who live here," she thought desperately. "There must be *some* way! I've just got to ride those horses."

"Oh, Grant!" called a woman's voice from the house. He set down his rake and walked off without a backward glance. Jane sat on the fence and thought, and the more she thought, the madder she

11

got. So Grant Davidson thought if you couldn't muck out a stall, you couldn't ride a horse.

"Of all the pig-headed, bad-tempered dopes!" she muttered, feeling thoroughly pig-headed and bad-tempered herself. "I'll show *him!*" She jumped down from the fence and pushed open the stable door. In a corner of the back room she found a pair of overalls hanging from a nail. They were much too big, but she stepped into them, rolled the pants up around the ankles, and seized the rake. She went to work where Grant had left off, raking out the trampled litter with vicious jabs. Then she scraped and smoothed the packed clay of the floor with the square-ended shovel. To her surprise, she found she was beginning to enjoy herself. She spread the clean, shining straw on the floor with as much care and pride as if she were setting a table for a dinner party.

It was not easy work. By the time she had finished the next stall, perspiration was dripping down her face, and there was a brand new blister at the base of her thumb, but she stepped back and surveyed her work with a glow of satisfaction. "What next?" she wondered. The water buckets needed filling. There was one in each stall, set into a bracket to keep the horses from overturning it. She tugged at one, but could not get it out.

"Like this," said Grant at her elbow, and handed her the bucket. "Use the faucet at the corner of the barn. Rinse the bucket well before you refill it." The full buckets were heavy, but she made the trip three times, raising another blister and slopping a good deal of water into her loafers.

"Now what?" she asked. Grant put down the bag of feed he was carrying.

"That's all," he said, grinning. Jane grinned back. "Look, Jane," he said, "I'm sorry I was so nasty, but I was in an awful temper this afternoon. I wanted to stay at school for the game—and I couldn't. So I took it out on you."

"I was in a sort of temper myself," admitted Jane. "So let's call it even. Oh—look!" The horses were crowding around the gate.

"They think it's dinner time," explained Grant. "If I don't let the gray one in, he'll come over the fence in a minute."

"I like the little bay best," said Jane. "Do you ride him much?"

"Sunny? I've handled him a lot. He's used to the feel of a saddle and bridle. He could be broken now by a lightweight, but he won't be up to my weight for another year."

"Oh!" breathed Jane. "I—I weigh ninety-seven pounds."

He looked her over appraisingly. "Say—that's an idea. Of course, I'd have to see you ride first. You need light hands for that job. Can you ride in those overalls?"

"I can ride in anything!" she cried.

"O.K. I'll saddle Lady for you, and I want you to watch while I do it, because next time, you're going to do it while *I* watch."

13

"Next time!" Jane's heart was singing as she vaulted into the saddle.

"Take her around the meadow a couple of times," Grant directed.

At first Jane rode stiffly, acutely conscious of Grant's critical eye on her. Her hands felt wooden, and getting a good knee grip in a pair of baggy overalls was a very different matter from riding in well-tailored breeches. But by the time Lady settled into a smooth canter, Jane had forgotten everything else in the world. Around and around the big meadow they swept. Jane could have gone on forever, but she pulled Lady down to a trot and returned triumphantly to the gate. Then she noticed the tall woman leaning on the fence beside Grant.

"Oh, my!" she thought in a sudden panic. "I bet she's mad at him for letting me ride her horse. Oh, what if he loses his job!"

But Grant was smiling and waving. As Jane jogged through the gate, Grant turned to the woman and said, "Mother, this is Jane McGregor. How about it—shall I let her break Sunny for me?"

Jane blushed and stammered something, as Mrs. Davidson said, "I'm very happy to meet you, Jane. I expect you could do a good job on Sunny—if you aren't afraid to take a few spills. Come up to the house, you two, when you're through, and we'll try to find something to eat."

Later, sitting on the porch with Grant and his mother, eating cake and drinking cold milk, Jane blurted out, "I—I thought Grant was the stable-boy."

14

"I am," he replied, through a large mouthful of cake. "Of course Dad helps on week ends."

"Grant has been in complete charge of the stable ever since we moved here," explained his mother. "It was that or give up the horses and move into an apartment. The only thing that worries me is the fact that he doesn't seem to have gotten acquainted with anyone at school yet."

"Well, gosh," complained Grant. "I have to rush right home after school. And then, most people are such dopes about horses. You can't very well walk up to a perfect stranger and say, 'Come on home with me this afternoon, and we'll have a fine time shoveling out a stable!'"

"I don't see why not!" exclaimed Jane, with spirit. "I'll come and shovel every day—that is, if you'll let me. And as for getting acquainted, *I* know what! You just come to my birthday party a week from tomorrow, and you'll get acquainted with the whole gang! They're a pretty good bunch, too," she added, "even if they are dopes about horses!"

As Jane bicycled home, protesting muscles told her that she would be stiff tomorrow, but she rode in a haze of happiness. She burst into the house, shouting, "Mother! Mother! Say, isn't it about time we did something about my party?"

"Your party?"

"Sure—it's my birthday next week. Don't I *always* have a party?"

Mrs. McGregor beamed. "Why, Jane, darling, I'm so glad you're taking an interest in things at last.

15

I was afraid you'd never stop mooning because you couldn't have a horse."

Jane threw her arms around her mother in a bear hug. "I don't have to moon any more about horses I haven't got," she caroled. "I've *got* horses—or just as good as! I can ride every single day, yes, and mess around the stable all I want. Golly, I've got to dig up my jodhpurs and some overalls that fit. And, jeepers, I'd better get on the phone and start rounding up the gang! How many may I ask? And I'll have to make up with Chuck first. I know, I'll ask him to bring Carol—she hasn't got a date for the Fall Dance yet. And, say, Mother—how about a new dress? Something that will just knock your eye out. There's a new boy coming, and he doesn't know anything about it yet, but I have a date with him for the Fall Dance!"

Storm

J. P. FOLINSBEE

IT was not yet daybreak. Laurie closed the screen door softly behind her and looked up, searching, at the sky. The morning star still glittered on the horizon, and the black chain of mountains to the west was just beginning to be gold-tipped by the unborn sun.

She shivered and put up the collar of her jacket. At least there was no threat of impending rain. All through yesterday's downpour, Storm had grown worse, as though the dampness had seeped into his bones and sent new waves of chill racing through him.

The thought brought back into sharp focus the frightening dream that had awakened her. It was better not to think about it. She had dreamed that Storm, fully saddled, had been running endlessly, desperately through sheets of torrential rain. She had been running after him, calling and calling, but he had not heard, and at last he had been swallowed in mist and she had fallen—only to waken in the dark.

It was foolish to dwell on it. Storm would surely feel better this morning. And with the veterinarian coming from Tamarack Junction, everything would be all right. It had to be! Probably they would all laugh about it afterward. It was probably nothing worse than a bad cold. . . .

She walked swiftly away from the ranchhouse, and cut past the dark outlines of the stable and the corral toward the west pasture. Her father had considered it best to isolate Storm from their other horses, and had helped her make a warm, comfortable bed for him in the small granary. With threshing still three weeks off, it made an ideal hospital.

She hurried. The thick late-August dew clung to the bottoms of her jeans, and turned the pastures to a ghostly silver in the failing darkness. It was going to be the kind of day Storm loved best—crisp and cool, with a tang of fall in the restless air. Perhaps by evening he would be up. . . .

The first time she had raced him on the open prairie had been just such a day. After two long months of breaking and holding him in, she had at last let him have his head, and he had streaked across the open range like a thunderbolt. How he loved it! Even as a colt four years ago, Storm had been like that—wild, spirited, forever trying to outrace the wind. And he had never lost that boldness. Until, suddenly, two days before, the strange sickness had swept over him.

She opened the granary door cautiously. A

lighted lantern hung from a rafter nail, and in the weird shadows she could see Storm lying in the straw, his proud head stretched out, his legs drawn up like a colt's. Her father was kneeling at his side, sponging down his forehead from a pail of water.

Laurie's throat tightened. Her father must have spent the night out here with Storm, while she selfishly slept. He had sent her to bed at midnight, promising to come soon, and she had fallen asleep while still listening for the sound of his footsteps. Probably he had never intended to sleep at all.

"Dad," she called, her voice carrying across Storm's heavy breathing. "Dad, is he all right?"

Her father looked up and smiled wearily. "Hello, Laurie." He managed a grin. "You beat the birds this morning." Tenderly he touched Storm's swollen shoulder. "I don't know. He seems about the same. No sudden cures by night. He's a game fellow, though."

Laurie knelt at her father's side, and stroked Storm's feverish muzzle. It was all so unbelievable. Just three days ago she had taken him for a twilight run to round up three stray cattle down by the river. He had been as eager and playful as a yearling, tossing his great white mane, insisting on splashing into the water and leaping back onto the bank to shake himself with enormous glee. She had never seen him more electric with life, and he hadn't even a sniffle that night.

Then, without warning, it had happened. In the morning she had found him standing dejectedly in his stall. Alarmed, she had felt his muzzle. It

19

had been raging with fever, and he had cried at her touch. She had run for her father, but he was as baffled as she. At first he thought it might be a touch of colic, or—as she thought—a cold from wading in the river waters. But now—Storm struggled to lift his head, and again the low, choked whinny escaped his throat.

"Easy, boy, easy," Laurie whispered. "Try to lie still." She rearranged his blanket and looked at her father. "He couldn't do that yesterday, Dad," she said. "He must be feeling better."

"Maybe. Maybe it's only that you're here with him, Laurie." He shook his head. "I don't want to sound discouraging. But I'm afraid Storm here may be a pretty sick fellow."

Laurie dipped the sponge and gently laved Storm's forehead with the cool water. *Her father must suspect something more than a cold. And in his own indirect way he was trying to prepare her —just in case. But it was so unreal. Storm was too young, too full of life. People got sick, too, but they recovered. Serious things didn't happen this way —overnight, with no warning at all.*

"Why don't you go back to the house, Dad, and rest," she said at last. "I'll stay here with him until the doctor comes. You must be worn out."

"All right, Laurie. Since you're up anyway." He rose stiffly. At the door he hesitated. "I'm sorry about this, Laurie," he said awkwardly. "I hope it is only a cold. But, well—whatever the doctor says, try to believe it's for the best, won't you?"

"Of course, Dad," she whispered. It was so un-

20

like him to say something so—so much a warning! She mustered a smile. "And thanks for staying up with him. I wish you had let me."

"Can't afford to have two sick youngsters around the place," he said with mock gruffness. "I'll come out and spell you at breakfast." He ducked down and was gone.

Laurie looked blankly after him for a moment, then turned back to Storm.

Sitting together in the darkness like this, it was almost like the night he had been born. A towering blizzard had swept down from the mountains that night, and snow was still buffering the stables when she had at last been able to see him at dawn.

"He's a storm baby, all right," her father had laughed. "I thought for sure this fellow was a goner. What a night!"

She had laughed, too—far too overwhelmed to talk. They had let her hold the colt's head in her hands for a moment, and he had nuzzled her arm. Even then she hadn't been quite able to believe that the tiny, rangy foal was hers—to own and to care for. He was her birthday gift, and he had come only a week from the day.

Finally, he had snorted noisily and frowned at her disapprovingly. She had laughed in delight, and then the idea had come to her.

"That's what we'll call him," she had cried. "*Storm!* That's his name."

"Storm," she whispered now, pushing his forelock back from his eyes. "Remember that night? Oh, Storm, try to get well. Try, boy, try. . . ."

21

The sun was riding upward when Laurie at last heard voices approaching over the fields.

". . . just two days ago," she heard her father say. "He seemed to fail all at once. Listless, legs weak, eyes cloudy with a yellowish film. But you'll see for yourself. It beats me."

They loomed in the doorway, her father towering a good six inches above the short, stocky frame of Dr. Herrick. He was much younger than Laurie had imagined, with a grave, friendly smile and a shock of wavy brown hair above dark-rimmed glasses which made him look more like a scientist than a veterinary.

"This is our daughter, Laurie," her father made the introductions. "Storm being her horse, she's the boss—so I'll turn you over to her."

"Well, Laurie," the doctor said when they had shaken hands. "That's a real handful of patient you have there."

Laurie's tension drained away. He understood—you could see it in his sympathetic glance at Storm. "That's right, doctor. He needs you very badly, I think," she ended lamely.

He smiled and set his medical kit against the wall.

"Well, let's hope not. First, suppose you tell me what you know. Your father has given me some information, but I'd like to know how you found him. How he acted before he got sick. Anything at all you noticed. Go back a week or so."

Carefully, Laurie retraced the hours she had been with him, their last exuberant ride, and Storm's insistence on splashing through the shallows of the river.

The doctor listened gravely.

"The river, you say? Was he overheated at the time?"

"No." Laurie frowned. "He'd waded hundreds of times before. It was a kind of game with him." She looked down. "He always got mad at me if I didn't let him go in."

"I see." The doctor shook his head. "Well," he said, "let's take a look."

Finally, Dr. Herrick rose, wiping his hands on a clean cloth. He turned to her. Even before he spoke, she knew it was bad from the expression in his gray eyes. It was funny, how a person's eyes betrayed his thoughts.

"I'm afraid he's a very sick horse," he said quietly. "I'll have to do a blood—and possibly an inoculation test to be absolutely certain—but I've seen a lot of these cases lately. It looks like acute infectious anemia."

"How bad is it, doctor? It doesn't mean—" Laurie left the question hang.

"Infectious anemia—or swamp fever—is a kind of malaria fever that horses get, Laurie," he elaborated. "It's quite common in certain parts of the country. In acute cases a horse sometimes—goes with it, very suddenly in the first attack. However, it isn't always fatal. Some horses survive an attack like this. Their fever breaks, and they seem to be as good as new."

Laurie's heart lifted and sank sharply as the true

meaning of his careful diagnosis broke through her first surge of gladness.

"*Seem* as good as new?" she echoed faintly.

He nodded soberly. "That's right, Laurie. The virus that causes the disease stays in their systems, just waiting to break out. Usually it's—well, a matter of fifteen to thirty days in serious cases." He paused and looked at Storm. "It's a rotten break, a beautiful animal like this. And there's one more thing. An animal with it can spread the infection to others, even though he, himself, may have seemed to recover."

"You mean Storm could make other horses sick —even if he got well?" Laurie's mind recoiled from the icy shock of his words.

"That's right. We call such animals chronic carriers. Swamp fever is one of the worst things we have to deal with." He sighed. "However, let's be very sure before we decide what to do."

He turned and took a hypodermic from his bag. "Let me do this blood test. Then we'll see. All right?"

"All right, doctor. And thank you—for telling me the truth."

It was more than an hour later when Andy Grey, their neighbor, appeared in the doorway.

"Hello, Laurie," he said. "I hope I didn't startle you."

"Hello, Mr. Grey." Laurie looked up. He seemed distraught and worried as he came in. "Is—is anything wrong? At your place, I mean?" A sudden

24

fear seized her that maybe his horses had been stricken.

"No." He shook his head. "No. Not a thing. How is he now?"

"About the same." She looked down. "He's been sleeping. I think his fever is down a little. I don't know really."

"It's a very great shame." His faint Scotch burr was soft with concern: "Your father and the doctor are down at the stables, Laurie. They'd like to talk with you, if you wouldn't mind my staying with him a bit."

Laurie walked slowly across the fields. The sun was intensely warm, and a few castled clouds had begun to build on the horizon. *It was almost certain what they would tell her. Storm was going to die. Dr. Herrick had said as much, already. Still, she could not believe it. The words were only words, her mind would never admit them to reality. It was today, and Storm was sick. But tomorrow—soon—he would be well. There must be a way. . . .*

Her father and Dr. Herrick were talking in Storm's stall.

As she hesitated in the stable doorway, their voices drifted back to her.

". . . scrubbed thoroughly with disinfectant," Dr. Herrick was saying. "Harness, stalls, floor, feed box—everything. Currycombs, brushes, blankets, any personal equipment it would be best to burn."

The blood drained from Laurie's heart. His words could mean only one thing.

Her father knocked his pipe out against his hand as she approached. She had never known him to look so tired—so worn and pale.

"I have something here I would like you to see, Laurie," Dr. Herrick took over quietly. He lifted a wire rack from the feed box and held it up to the window. In it were two test tubes, one bright red, the other pale and watery.

"I guess I don't have to tell you that this one" —he indicated the pale column—"is Storm's blood. The other is from a healthy animal." He paused. "There's the whole story, Laurie."

"Then—then there's nothing you can do?" she asked, suddenly calm.

"There's no known treatment," Dr. Herrick said carefully. "Not yet, at least. So I'm going to ask you to take my place, Laurie. I want you to be the doctor from now on."

"I—I don't understand." Her voice faltered. *Did he mean there was—somewhere—a shadow of hope?*

Dr. Herrick's voice interrupted her whirling thoughts. "If Storm recovers from this attack— which he might—he might have days, even a few weeks. No one can say for sure. He will never be entirely well again. But he might live—exist—until the next attack or the next."

"Then he won't—won't have to be destroyed?"

"Well," Dr. Herrick hesitated. "I've already explained the considerable danger to your other horses. But there's no law that says Storm must be

26

destroyed." He paused. "That is what I want you to decide."

Laurie looked desperately at her father. But his gaze was fastened on the window. It was all so bewildering.

Her father turned at last. "There's one other thing, Laurie," he said. "Something Dr. Herrick hasn't explained to you, but he has been doing considerable experimental work on this particular disease—trying to find something that will really kill the virus that causes it and be a true cure. It's extremely important work."

Their eyes met and held, and suddenly, clearly, she understood. Now she knew what Dr. Herrick had meant when he had asked her to be the doctor. She turned to him.

"You do want to destroy Storm, then," she said slowly.

He nodded. "Not only for my work, Laurie. But in every way, as a doctor, I think it would be best."

"Would it—would it help other horses? If you took Storm now, I mean? Would it really help you to find a cure?" The words slipped out almost against her will.

"It's like a chain, Laurie. Each new case is a link. But no one can say where the chain will end. That's how it is."

"I see." It was so unreal, as though they were discussing some scientific animal she didn't know at all. Even here, in the very stall where Storm had grown up, his presence was strong, and yet

27

somehow remote, like the Storm she had run after in her dream. . . .

"Don't try to decide now, Laurie." Her father's voice, too, seemed far off. "Why don't you take a little walk outside. Think about it. Whatever you decide will be best, you know that."

She glanced up gratefully. How could he always sense when she was on the verge of tears?

"All right, Dad. I'll—I'll be all right in a minute."

She walked swiftly from the stall and ran toward the bright patch of day framed by the doorway.

Outside, the sun caught her up in all its brilliance. The sky was filling swiftly with clouds, great turreted ships adrift on a turbulent blue sea.

In every way, as a doctor, I think it would be best.

It wasn't fair. He was asking her to think of Storm as just another sick animal, not as someone she knew and loved.

If Storm had to go, he should go here, among familiar things, in his own way, close to people who loved him. Storm had a great heart. He wouldn't be afraid when the time came. Even if he knew, he wouldn't be afraid at all. . . .

The thought turned, slipped away, and drifted back. *If he knew.* She hadn't thought of it in that way. How would Storm feel, if he was the one that had to decide? Not afraid, that was sure. But would he want to wait for death to come? Or would he want to go as he had lived, plunging out to meet it, gallantly, recklessly—trying to outrace the wind.

Dr. Herrick wouldn't lie. He was sure Storm had

only days at best. Painful days, with intervals of dull relief—until at last he slipped away on an adventure she could not share. *And, in her heart, did she have any right to hold him, to lengthen his suffering, only because she could not bear to lose him?*

A gust of wind blew sharp and cold against her face. She looked up, startled. The clouds were massing swiftly now, sending dark, streaming shadows across the grass. A rumble of thunder sounded its warning in the sky.

Her breath caught. They would have to hurry. Within an hour, the storm was bound to break in all its fury. . . .

Laurie lay wide awake against the pillow, listening to the drums of thunder and rain crashing against the roof. Her arms and legs ached with weariness, but she could not sleep. There was so much to remember of this day, to make a part of memory forever. . . .

The sudden storm, coming and sweeping like swift, dark wings across the earth. And Storm himself, who would now give all storms their meaning. He had gone so quietly, as though he understood, and was glad. . . .

And it was best, of course. Storm had given his life. But in giving it, he might restore life to unknown generations of his kind. Even if the search took years, they would find a way. And she would always remember him, not as he was when the sick-

29

ness came, but as he had been on that last, unfor-
gettable ride.

She turned restlessly toward the window. In its
black depths you could imagine—almost see—the
shadows of the angry clouds twisting in the sky.
Storm would have loved this night.

The door opened quietly, and Laurie looked up
in alarm. It was her father, clad in a still-dripping
slicker. He was carrying a hurricane lantern in his
hand.

"Dad!" Laurie sat up in panic. "What's the matter? Is—is one of the other horses sick?"

"No," he reassured her. "I just came from Andy
Grey's," he explained. "I thought I'd take a chance
that you would still be awake."

"What's happened?" she whispered. He seemed
so excited, with the tiredness completely gone from
his face.

"Andy called just after you had gone to bed," he
said. "You remember when he came over this afternoon? Well, I didn't like to tell you then—but that
mare of his was getting restless."

Her hands grew as cold as ice. "Which mare,
Dad?"

"There's only one I would waken you to tell you
about tonight, Laurie," he smiled. "It probably
wouldn't have happened for three or four days, in
the normal course of things. But when the storm
started, she got frightened, and things started moving—fast."

"Dad!" Laurie seized his arm. "Not—not—?"

"That's right." He grinned at her. "Storm's son.

He was born less than an hour ago." He looked down at her. "You don't know how I wanted to help you by telling you about it this afternoon, Laurie. I'm glad I didn't, now. Andy wanted you to know—Storm's colt is yours, of course."

She stared up at him, still not able to believe it. Then, at last, after the long day of holding back, her tears came. She looked away out toward the raging night, but her hand crept into his as a tremendous flash of lightning illuminated the sky and the earth and vanished into blackness before the thunder came.

No Sum Too Small

◆━━━◆━━━◆━━━◆━━━◆

MURRAY HOYT

THE whole thing took place in two weeks during the year Jeanie Williams was fifteen years old. For her they were two hard weeks. By the end of those two weeks, when the letter came saying that the thing Jeanie had hoped for was to be given to someone else, she was changed. You did not see the change; she was the same quiet, polite, serious person. But you felt the change. She wasn't a little girl any more after that letter came; she was older, more mature. She was a small adult.

The first day of that two weeks I met her in front of my house. Her face was serious as always, trying to hide the way she felt, but her eyes danced and her step was so light it was almost as if she were dancing.

She said, "Look, Uncle Red—look at this."

She handed me a little magazine called Horsemanship. She pointed to an ad which said that a woman in Massachusetts wanted to find a home for a hunter she wanted to retire, where it would be cared for well and treated with kindness and affection. The woman could not keep it because she did not have stable room and had acquired a younger horse to take its place. She did not want to sell it because she wanted the right to check carefully on the character of the person who got it, and to receive reports on how it was being treated. She also wanted to control absolutely any later transfer of ownership.

Jeanie had been reading the ad as I read it and she said very softly, almost reverently, "It says 'kindness and affection.'" Then she looked full at me and she added a little louder, "It sounds almost as if she was describing me. It seems almost as if I'm the one she's talking about."

I said, "Are you going to apply, Jeanie?"

She said, nodding eagerly, "Oh, yes. Dad and Mother say I can. It's the first time they've ever agreed to anything like that. I told them that if I got it, the money I've saved toward a horse could go for tack, for shipping the horse up here and for the expense of taking care of him. A year from now I'll be old enough to get a summer job that will give me the money to keep a horse another whole year."

I watched her walking away primly, on her way to school. Under the primness I could sense that terrific excitement that made me expect that at any second her walk might become a dance.

I watched her and I thought that probably Joe and Mildred Williams, her parents, couldn't very well have said anything but yes.

But I knew that it was a mistake. I knew the terrific hurt that was coming to Jeanie when the horse was given to someone else. That magazine was read in horse circles all over the United States. It wasn't reasonable to suppose, even before the letter came, that Jeanie would be the chosen one. . . .

Kids long for things inexplicable to an adult. In Jeanie's case it was a horse. Literally, more than anything else in the world, Jeanie wanted a horse. It wasn't the "Daddy, buy me a pony" sort of thing that all kids go through; it started when she was very small, when Mr. Brown used to put her on old Duffer's back to ride from the barn to the pasture gate, and it grew and grew.

She believed that if you wanted a thing badly enough and worked hard enough for it, you'd get it. And she never lost faith that sometime the good break would come. She was a religious little kid, as much as any kid fifteen years old is religious, and she believed that God would not let her down in this matter because He alone could know how much it meant to her.

We who lived near her were rooting for her because she was a nice kid, friendly in spite of being a little on the quiet side, and because I suppose Americans always root for the underdog.

We were practical and we'd seen an awful lot of people with a faith as clear and shining as Jeanie's taste the deep bitterness of disillusion.

She asked for a horse her sixth Christmas when she made out her list for Santa Claus. It was the only item on the list.

Joe and Mildred explained to her that a horse was a very expensive present, that Santa Claus probably knew they had no place to keep a horse, and nothing to feed one. They suggested that she ask for other things in case Santa Claus should feel it best to substitute.

She said, "But he won't do that, because a horse is the only thing I want."

There were some grand presents on Christmas Day. Jeanie was very polite and appreciative. But she grew quieter and quieter all the time they were giving out presents. When they were all through, she disappeared and they knew she had gone somewhere alone to cry.

Joe felt horrible. If there'd been any way in the world he could have swung a pony for her, he'd have done it then. But he was a college professor in the little Vermont college at Mead. During the depression, college professors took a cut and he just didn't have the money to swing it. In addition Mildred had had a lot of hospital expenses when the second child was born, and they were expecting another baby. Joe was paying for his house. And to add to everything else, that house was in a development restricted to household pets. It didn't help much to know that all those things were true when he also knew that Jeanie was somewhere alone bawling her eyes out.

She never asked for a horse again. In fact beginning about then she developed the habit of not asking for anything she wasn't positive she'd receive. She'd go to amazing lengths to hint around and find out whether the answer would be yes before she actually asked. She seemed to dread being refused. That first time must have been very bad.

Joe and Mildred sat back after that and waited for Jeanie to forget the horse business, and they thought this was happening until the tin box appeared on her bureau. It had a piece of brown sticker tape pasted on the cover and on that was printed HORS MUNNE. Inside were her two bankbooks, started by the two grandmothers when she was born, a dollar her grandfather had given her for Christmas, the quarter which comprised her last week's allowance, and a penny which she had found in the big chair after the insurance man had called.

Mildred called Joe in and showed it to him. He looked at it thoughtfully. He asked about the penny and she told him.

He said, "No sum too small."

And Mildred said, "But, Joe, the amount is pitiful and absurd compared to what a horse would cost. She's so ignorant of what she's up against. She's going to be so bitterly disappointed. We've got to make her see just how impossible it would be for a little girl to save that much money."

They waited until the time was right, and then Mildred had a long talk with Jeanie. She explained that Jeanie could not buy a horse for much less than a hundred and fifty dollars. She tried to make her understand how many one-dollar-and-twenty-six-centses it would take to make a hundred and fifty dollars.

Jeanie listened to her and seemed to understand, but the box remained on the bureau, and the next time Mildred looked there was more money in it.

They didn't always know where Jeanie got the money, unless they asked her. But we neighbors knew. It became noised around that Jeanie would, at fifteen cents an hour, do practically anything after school and Saturdays within her strength and ability. And there were a surprising number of errands to be run, trips to the store, hickory nuts to be shucked—things like that. She'd take the nickel or dime, and she'd thank you primly and then she'd start to walk away. Only after a few steps it would be too much for her and she'd run, as if she could hardly wait to reach that tin box.

Mildred saw her put the money in, once. There was really a little ceremony to it. First she opened the box and stirred the contents a little with her hand. Then she held the new piece of money a foot or so above the box to make it clink satisfyingly when it dropped in. After she dropped it, she carefully closed the lid again.

She loved every horse within a mile of home, and some a lot farther away than that. This included several specimens of flea bait definitely not worth loving by any but Jeanie's all-embracing standards.

And all the horses loved her. When she was a little kid still, I used to watch her from my window make a beeline for old Duffer's pasture fence. And he'd trot right over and put his head down to be petted. She'd stroke him and lay her face against him, feel his soft nose. And when he grew tired of this, she'd follow him around and squat beside him to watch him eat. You'd see her lips moving and you knew she was carrying on a one-sided, animated conversation with him. When she was called back to the house, he would follow her to the pasture fence and stand looking after her as she made for home with that sturdy businesslike walk which is peculiar to small children. Duffer never paid any attention to anyone else who came near his pasture.

As the time passed between her sixth and thirteenth years, her character began to take shape. I believed, and Joe and Mildred agreed, that wanting this one thing as much as she did probably had a considerable effect in forming it. She was a gentle kid, never cruel. She was quiet, and while she had a grand smile and you knew when she was happy, she was never boisterous in happiness. In fact all emotion, especially hurt, she hid very successfully from grownups, seeming to prefer to fight it out all alone.

She had a lot of friends but no very close companion as most girls that age seem to have. She was extremely affectionate. She was perhaps more affectionate toward her parents than the average child, and the rest spilled out lavishly among the horses she knew, and among all other animals of her acquaintance indiscriminately.

The Fergusons' horse, Perry, Jeanie rode a lot and fussed with a lot. Mary Ferguson was afraid of it, and Perry was not always completely sold on Mr. Ferguson. The result was that occasionally they could not catch their animal and had to come to Jeanie for help.

Jeanie would walk out there into the pasture and she would call with that serious, grown-up manner of hers, "Perry, you've been a very bad boy. Now you come here this instant."

And Perry would come. He'd trot over with a happy little whinny and docilely allow the halter to be slipped over his head, though a few minutes before he had been galloping from one end of the pasture to the other with a great show of heels when anyone tried to approach him. This I saw with my own eyes. Why it was so, I don't know, unless a horse has some way of knowing who loves him and who doesn't.

She began going out to Helen Blair's when she was ten. Helen Blair lived a couple of miles outside town and owned a stable of riding horses. In the summer she furnished both horses and instruction to a girls' camp on the other side of the state. The rest of the year she gave lessons there at home. Trust Jeanie to find out about a setup like that. The couple of times I'd been out there the place had seemed to be infested with little girls, feeding, currying, saddling horses, and riding endlessly around a ring. And looking at me with polite condescension when I asked what "tack" was and what "posting" meant.

I gathered from Jeanie that, to the little girls who liked riding and horses, it was like a club out there. And they adored Helen. When they didn't have money for a lesson, they hung around anyway.

Jeanie spent most of her time out there. Helen said she used to spend hours just standing in the stalls brushing the horses; sometimes just talking to them.

She took to getting up early and doing her hour of piano practice before school. She'd do her room work at noon, then after school she'd ride out to Helen's on her bicycle. In the evening she'd study and go to bed early so that she could get up for the practicing the next morning.

I saw her out there once and complimented her on her riding. She thanked me carefully. But I watched her eyes. They were looking past me at two girls from the town below who owned their own little Morgans. If I ever read loneliness and longing in anyone's eyes it was in hers then.

When I turned away I knew that with her, the riding, the lessons, the having other people's horses come to her, was all very well. But there was a big, lonely void that only having her own horse to love and fuss over could ever fill.

I used to ask her once in a while how the horse fund was coming along. Sometimes she'd say, "Oh, pretty good." But sometimes she would tell me something definite and I would know that she wanted to talk to someone about it. That was the

41

way it was during the war when she gave the five dollars to the Red Cross.

She said, "It didn't seem right that I should be keeping all this money when the Red Cross was giving plasma and things to soldiers. It didn't seem right."

Yet you could sense the sacrifice it had been, the major setback to her hopes. She gave to the Red Cross three times and she bought war-savings stamps. But the stamps could go into the tin box, which was very heavy now. It was the same box that she had used right along, but now the HORS MUNNE had been crossed out and over it written, in a little girl's hand, HORSE MONEY.

By the time she was thirteen she was official baby tender for the neighborhood. The money always went into the tin box.

In a way it was too bad she liked ice cream and all kinds of sweets as much as she did because if she hadn't, saving would have been a lot easier. There must have been some pretty hard-fought battles behind that serious little face.

But always the tin box won out. There were only two things that she would spend money on; one was movies which had horses in them (and she saw all of those) and riding lessons at Helen's. Mostly she was able to get her dad or her mother to pay for the riding lessons but sometimes she could not, and then she very reluctantly tapped the fund. By that year when she was thirteen, she had almost one hundred dollars.

That was the year she began to grow tall. She had been a chubby little thing earlier, but suddenly she began to shoot up and all her hems were let out in a desperate effort to keep her properly clothed. I had expected she would be displeased at this sudden shooting upward, but I found her philosophical.

"It's much easier to mount now, Uncle Red."

The fourteenth year was when the pin-up boy appeared on her wall.

"It made me feel old," Joe said. "Here was my daughter starting to put up boys' pictures. It made me feel darned peculiar. So when the time was right I said to her, 'I was in your room today, Jeanie, and I noticed that Roy Rogers is your pin-up boy.' And she said, 'Oh, Daddy, that isn't Roy Rogers' picture. That's a picture of Trigger, his horse.'"

That was the year she found out about an old Morgan that could be had for one hundred and twenty-five dollars and she hinted around to find out whether Joe and Mildred would lend her the extra twenty-five dollars to buy it.

That was a fairly tough decision on all concerned. Joe could have stood the twenty-five without any trouble, but the upkeep he just wasn't financially able to handle. By that time inflation in the United States was a healthy urchin, and people with fixed salaries were pinched unmercifully under such conditions. Joe got out a pencil and a piece of paper and he began to write down the things they would need. Jeanie had an old catalogue and they looked up saddle, bridle, and probably other items which I know nothing about. Then he wrote down the everyday expenses that owning a horse would entail. There was stable rental, hay, oats, bran, shavings for bedding, pasture rental; a lot of other items like that. He said that as he wrote, Jeanie's face grew more and more expressionless. The animation drained from it and it became stoical.

They came to the conclusion that they would need at least seventy-five dollars for equipment (which Jeanie called tack) and that it would cost about one hundred dollars a year—at a conservative estimate—to take care of the horse.

Jeanie saw how impossible it was once the figures were down on paper. She thanked Joe for going over it with her, and excused herself. She didn't appear for a long time. They knew where she was, well enough, and Joe says he and Mildred both felt horrible. Jeanie was older now and very seldom went away by herself any more, the way she used to. It had to be something out of the ordinary to make her do that now.

I saw her a few days later and I asked her how the fund was coming. That was one of the times she told me something definite.

She explained about the cost of upkeep and of tack and everything. She said a little wistfully, "Sometimes, Uncle Red, I get very discouraged. I guess I'm going to be an old lady before I get my horse. I guess it will be so late it won't do me much good."

I said, "But you aren't going to give up, are you?"

And she said, "No, I'm not going to give up." Her jaw seemed to stick out a little when she said it, though that might have been my imagination.

That was the way things stood when the advertisement appeared in Horsemanship. As I have said, by that time everybody knew about Jeanie and her horse, and all of us were rooting for her. Two different people brought her the ad.

Jeanie applied. It was a nice straightforward letter with only a few misspelled words. Spelling had never been Jeanie's forte.

The weakness in the letter lay in the fact that Jeanie could not describe either the stable or the pasture, but had to say that if the horse were given to her she would have to look around and hire each of these items.

After the letter went off, everyone concerned sat back and waited. I'd see Jeanie walking to school and back and I could sense the tremendous excitement in her. She tried as always to hide any emotion she felt, but this was something out of the ordinary so that I could see it in the way she skipped along, in the way her eyes sparkled, in every move she made.

And my heart went out to her because I knew she couldn't win; I knew she couldn't because I was practical and figured the odds; they were many times a hundred to one against her.

She began to get together tack. She bought a pail to water the horse. She went down to the feed store and found out about oats and bran. She canvassed the street nearest our development for a stable. She poked into old barns, carriage houses, stalls. Everything is new in our development, but on Middle Street, which is next to ours, the houses have been there, many of them, for over a hundred years. Some of them have large barns and stables. She finally landed one of these. Then she went looking for a pasture. She spent two or three days on this. She had trouble finding one near enough to the stable, but she stuck to it in her grave, polite little way and finally she succeeded. You went into her room and you found lists of horsy things she'd have to buy. The mail contained at least one catalogue for her every day.

You watched the excitement in her and your heart went out to her because you knew that she was building up to a disappointment which would shake her through and through, which would hurt her worse than she had ever been hurt in her life. You sensed that. You wished there were some way you could protect her, you could help her—yet you knew of nothing anyone could do.

When people talked to me downtown I found myself sticking up for her. One man said to me, "That is the luckiest thing I ever heard of. Sitting back and having a horse turned over to you."

I said, "I don't call it luck. In the first place it hasn't been turned over to her and probably won't be. But if it should be, it still isn't lucky. She's fought for it for years. She's had some tough breaks. A good break should be about due her. If she doesn't get this particular horse in this particular way, she'll get another one in a year or so because she's working for it all the time. It's the same sort of luck you might accuse a prospector of having when he's studied and worked for months, even years, and finally finds the gold a little quicker than he expected. It's one of those breaks you make yourself."

The guy looked at me surprised. He said, "Okay. You don't have to get so vehement about it. If you say so, it isn't luck."

Maybe I was touchy because I hated to see it happen to her. Sure she would get a horse in another year or so. To an adult a year is not very long. To a child it stretches away endlessly. When you're fifteen, a year is a long, long time. I wanted her to have the horse now.

It was during this period that Joe heard her praying. He went in to tuck her in for the night and open her window, and before he stepped off the carpet he heard her talking. Her eyes were tight shut and she was asking God to help her, to guide her. She had done everything she could do; now she needed help. He tiptoed back downstairs without going into the room.

She didn't say much about the mail but she went down to the post office every time a train came in, if she was free. And when she came home from school her eyes always went to the table where Joe and Mildred left the incoming letters.

At the end of two weeks the letter came. It was a short letter. It thanked her for her application but it said that under the circumstances, since she had neither stable nor pasture, the horse couldn't very well be turned over to her.

You didn't have to ask her what was in the letter. She drew into herself, and before she finished reading, her face was a mask. She stood there with the letter in her hand for a little while and once Joe thought she was going to drop it. But then she very quietly handed it to him. She wouldn't let them see her eyes.

She said, and her voice was thin and high-pitched, "Well, I'll have all these things ready anyway, when I do get one." Her voice didn't sound very natural. She was around for the next few minutes but after that they couldn't find her for a long, long time.

I guess Joe felt almost as badly as she did. He came over to see me, ostensibly to get any ideas I could give him, but I guess in reality he needed to get it off his chest. He told me that Mildred had phoned Helen for the same reason.

After Joe went back home I sat in the living room thinking about it. I thought about the hours of baby-tending and the running errands, I thought about the money gradually growing in the tin box on the bureau. I thought about Duffer following her across the pasture. I thought about her catching Perry when nobody else could lay a hand on him. I thought about her first pin-up boy, about her seeing National Velvet five complete times and parts of two others. She was just a little girl who wanted a horse very badly. And pretty soon I didn't feel very good inside. This had been her big chance. She had had faith, and having faith she had dropped her guard. Now she was hurt as she might never be hurt again. For my money it was a shame and if nobody could do anything about it at least a try could be made.

I picked up the telephone. I put in a person-to-person call to the lady in Massachusetts. The operator said, "I am sorry, sir, there will be a delay. That same call has just been put in by another party."

So I sat around and waited and I began to feel no better fast. I knew Jeanie would be away somewhere alone by that time, and little pictures of Jeanie in the past five years kept passing before my eyes.

After a while the phone rang and they told me that they had my party.

I told the lady who I was, and then I started in. I told her about Jeanie; what she looked like, all the things I knew about her. I told her about those first rides on Duffer, about that first Christmas, about Duffer following her around, about Perry, about the way she mothered all animals, about the tin box and its slow, slow accumulations, about the money to the Red Cross, about the capacity to love some horse, pet it, make over it, more than any horse was ever loved or made over before.

I said, "You want care and affection for your horse; you can never find them in such quantity anywhere again." I told her everything. She didn't interrupt me much. When I got through her voice sounded a little different. She thanked me for calling and then she told me something about the horse. His name was Topper. He was a grandson of Man o' War—by Thunderer out of a range mare. He was thirteen years old but still very sound. The only strings attached to her offer were that he must not be hunted, or ridden for hire, and must never be sold. If the person who got him could no longer keep him he must be returned. She said that Topper liked to be petted and would stand for hours and be curried. If he liked you he would follow you around. I gathered that Topper was lonesome, now that his place had been taken by another horse.

I said to her, "They're two of a kind. Jeanie has been lonely for a long time, for a horse to love. And Topper is lonely for a mistress to love him."

After that I hung up. When I got the bill later, the call cost me eight dollars and thirty-five cents. I figured I never spent eight dollars and thirty-five cents that I begrudged any less.

I found out afterward that Helen had called just ahead of me. That Massachusetts woman must have learned an awful lot about Jeanie in an awfully short time; though maybe we duplicated to some extent. If I had known about Helen's call I wouldn't have put in mine because I would have felt that as one horse woman to another, she could probably swing more weight than I could. I was just a guy who wanted to see a little girl get her horse.

Joe said that Jeanie was very quiet all evening. In the middle of the evening the phone rang and it was a telegram for her. It said: TOPPER IS YOURS. AM STARTING HIM OFF BY VAN YOUR EXPENSE EARLY TOMORROW MORNING. MAY I COME UP SOMETIME AND RIDE WITH YOU? And it was signed by the lady in Massachusetts.

Jeanie didn't mean to show how she felt any more when she knew the horse was hers than she had when she had thought it never would be. But she came tearing into the living room, her eyes big. Her whole face shone. Her whole body was light, as if she were hardly touching the ground.

They called me over and she had calmed down by then; but I have never seen anyone look so quietly radiant as she did. Joe said that all the next morning she whistled and sang. He said she was so happy that it was all around her like a halo. It wasn't that she had ever been unhappy; she had always been a happy kid. It was just that she had wanted something very, very badly and now she had it and she was so happy she couldn't begin to contain it.

It had to show itself somehow and so she hummed and sang and whistled all day.

At ten-thirty that night Helen called and said that the horse was there and was grand; big and lovable. The next morning I took them out before breakfast, because Joe's car wouldn't start.

She got out there and she walked into the stall

and up to his head, and he whinnied a little, softly, and nuzzled her with his velvety nose.

And she stroked him and held her cheek against him.

A Touch of Arab

VIVIAN BRECK

USUALLY the day we rode into the canyon to open the ranger cabin was the happiest of the whole year. On that day my father stopped being Professor Mallory of the Geology Department and changed into Ranger Mallory of Merced Canyon —and I had Cirque to ride. After a little time in the Sierra Nevada you get used to the light, but on the day you ride in, the sun seems so near and shines so gold-and-silver bright, that it stirs you up inside. The mountains have a sparkle on them.

Always before—and that's eleven summers, because we have been going to the Merced cabin ever since my mother died when I was three— Ranger Mallory's eyes would get sort of big behind his glasses and the tip of his nose would quiver at the smell of wild azaleas in Little Yosemite. He'd crack silly jokes as we rode and call himself "Old Sourdough." But this year he looked as if he had just flunked one of his favorite students.

"Look at Cirque, Daddy," I said. "Isn't he beautiful? He's so glad to be out of pasture he wants to dance uphill." Cirque is Western stock horse with just a touch of Arab. That makes him strong and dependable and brave, but a little flashy, too—he likes to prance.

But Daddy didn't seem to appreciate Cirque's polished granite coat and lovely legs. Surely, I thought, after we climb the zigzags and get to foaming water, or to where we can see the Clark Range, he will get his mountain face. The Clark Range looks like black starched fringe combed straight up against the sky. We think it's very exciting.

It was when we stopped for lunch that Daddy told me. We had built a cooking fire and were waiting for the water to boil for tea when he said, "I wish you'd stop trying to balance yourself on that branch, Meggie. I really don't want an acrobat for a daughter. Besides, I need to talk to you." He kept digging at the damp crust of pine needles on the ground as he spoke. "I'm sorry, Meg, but this is going to be a mighty short summer."

"What on earth do you mean?" I asked him. "It's not even July yet."

"But this year I'm having just a two-weeks' businessman's vacation." He put his hand on my arm. "Meg, my dear," he said almost pleadingly, "I do hope you'll understand." Then he told me that he had resigned from the Forest Service to accept a job teaching at summer session, and that he wanted me to go to a girls' camp.

"I don't want you growing up one-sided," he

said, "with no interests outside of your riding. You must cultivate other enthusiasms. You need friendship with boys and girls your own age. That's why I want you to go to this camp and make an honest effort to get along with the other girls and join in all their different activities."

"But Cirque!" I cried. "Darling Cirque! What will we do—"

"A professor's salary is not designed to include boarding a horse in town," Daddy answered slowly. "I'm sorry, but I think the time has come when we'll have to sell Cirque. Surely you wouldn't want to keep an educated young gentleman at pasture indefinitely. Would you, Meggie?"

I shook my head, but deep inside I knew there was more behind this selling Cirque than just money. Several times that spring I had cut school to practice for the gymkhana, and when Daddy found out about it he'd looked pretty grim.

"Education," he had said to me, his jaw particularly square, "is the bones of life. Without it you may grow up bright and pretty, but sometime life will crumble on you because you haven't the right bones underneath."

"Why do you have to be a professor all over your private life?" I'd railed. "You know I'm going to live on a ranch and raise stock horses. What's analyzing the 'Merchant of Venice' got to do with that?"

"Quite a lot," Daddy had said, and I knew there was no use arguing with him.

After that miserable lunch on the trail we rode

the rest of the fourteen miles to our cabin trying to talk about things that wouldn't hurt too much. But as we passed the granite slide where the Merced tumbles down in foaming sheets of water, I couldn't help remembering old Mr. Scripps.

"Did they ever find him?" I had to ask.

"Yes, they did," Daddy answered, as if rushing water were no longer beautiful. "At the bottom of Nevada Falls. There will be one advantage to our short summer, anyhow."

"How could there be?"

"I probably won't have to hunt for any lost fishermen or campers."

Usually when we arrive at the Ranger Station I want to squeal for joy. Our brown log cabin looks so welcoming, under the Jeffrey pines! This year I could only wonder whose name would be tacked up on the bulletin board where the little metal sign, "Ranger Arthur B. Mallory," had hung for so long. Cirque was all for dashing upstream to see if the big bridge, where the Lyell Fork joins the Merced, had lasted out the winter. Since the trail gang put a concrete pier under the bridge it has never washed out, but before that, every time we had a heavy storm the melted snow, swirling down in torrents from the upper falls, had carried the bridge with it. I unsaddled Cirque and turned him into the corral beside the cabin, then went inside to unpack. What I really wanted to do was bury my face in a pillow, or run across the river on my log and crawl into the underbrush, where the does hide their new fawns.

It was silly for Daddy to think that getting rid of Cirque would make me spend more time with what he calls "comrades of my own age." Those dopes! Last year he practically drove me to join a sort of dancing club. The dancing part wasn't bad—dancing is pretty good exercise. But the girls were so silly and the boys so juvenile in their conversation, I only went once. But it had never occurred to me that my not going to dances, and being bored by my schoolmates, would get mixed up in Daddy's mind with my loving Cirque so much. How could I make him understand the way I felt about my darling? My father wouldn't sell me, no matter how much I cost to keep!

Suddenly an idea hit me. Cirque looks especially beautiful standing on his hind legs or jumping. If, every day for two weeks, Daddy had to watch my horse doing extra-special, prancy tricks, perhaps—

I raced into the cabin for my lucky tee shirt—the blue-and-white striped one I wore when I won the bareback hackamore race at the gymkhana. Then I jerked the top bars off the corral gate, and made Cirque jump so that every muscle showed under his glossy coat. Finally, to rest him, we practiced a kind of circus trick I have been wanting to learn. That was when Wake came along.

Right next to our cabin is a mammoth Jeffrey pine with one branch overhanging the corral. I stood on Cirque's back (that isn't hard if you have grippy toes and are used to climbing over logs) and swung myself to the overhanging branch. The hard part was dropping down again on Cirque's back while he was loping by. I was riding around standing up when I spotted something that looked like a great blue heron—all legs, with a hump on top—leaning against the corral, one of his legs wound around the other. When I rode over, the hump turned out to be a knapsack, and the heron asked, "Can I take a picture of you doing that stunt? You're a wonderful color. Like the ocean— extremely clean blue-and-white."

"I don't mind," I said, wondering whether he meant that my shirt looked like the ocean, or my face. My eyes are violently blue, and my eyebrows and hair looked mighty pale against my sun-browned skin.

While he set up a tripod, Cirque and I did our trick over and over.

"What's your horse's name?" he asked.

"Cirque."

"Circ, for circus?"

"Circus nothing! He's a mountain horse. His name is C-i-r-q-u-e. Don't you know any geology? A cirque is the round place hollowed out of the granite at the head of a stream by a glacier. You ought to study geology," I told him. "It makes the mountains much more interesting."

He said he doubted if he'd ever have time.

That was Wake. His whole name was Wakefield Bender. He was seventeen, and this was his first trip into the Sierra Nevada. He had heard that the Merced, just below the Ranger cabin, was full of cascades running between granite cliffs, and he thought they would make interesting pictures.

Daddy suggested I help him choose a place to camp. It was lucky I did. Wake didn't know any more about the woods than I know about photography.

"This looks like a fine place to hang my hat," he announced at the place where the trail crossed Rafferty Creek, two minutes from our cabin. "I'd like to wake up in the morning looking at those big black rocks sticking out through the bubbles."

"You'll wake up in a puddle, if it rains," I told him. "Rafferty catches a tremendous runoff. It spreads out all over the place after a shower."

As he was looking back at the foam of water he stumbled and nearly went flat. If I had known how easy it was for Wake to stumble I never would have cut through the woods on a deer trail! He laughed about his clumsiness, though, even when a rock sent him sprawling. I couldn't help laughing, too. He looked so silly with his heron legs waving in the air.

"Your legs remind me of Alice and her neck," I said. "They've grown so fast you don't know how to manage them."

"Quick!" he shouted. "Find me a mushroom to nibble!"

After that we were easy together. Somehow, when people too old for fairy tales both like "Alice in Wonderland" it gives them the feeling of being old friends.

The place I had in mind for Wake's camp didn't

suit him at all. "This has no character," he objected.

"But look at the firewood! And it has perfect screening from the wind."

He still shook his head. "It's just shrubbery. I want to camp where the outlook has form—composition of some kind. A picture to live with."

Finally he made camp on a granite shelf, where little crooked pines grow out of the cracks in the rock. As I watched him unpack I hoped he had food in his knapsack as well as camera stuff, because he was awfully thin. You could see his shoulder blades right through his shirt. I couldn't help liking him. He had nice brown eyes that looked straight at you—that is, when one of them wasn't covered up with a piece of rumply hair. I asked him why he didn't get a haircut before he came away.

"There wasn't time," he said. "And anyhow, I'd spent all my allowance on film."

Wake walked over to our cabin quite often to watch me jumping Cirque, and sometimes I rode past his camp to tell him about something I thought he might like to photograph. I never picked the things he wanted, though. It was the cascades that fascinated him. They were difficult to photograph because the canyon walls are so steep, and he was anxious to explore the other side of the river for a better angle, so one day I showed him where my log crosses. My log—I call it mine because I've used it so many years—is the only way over the Merced between our cabin and the big junction bridge five miles upstream. Wake said he wished he could skitter about fallen trees the way I do. His legs reminded me of a colt's—they wouldn't quite obey him.

We had several conversations before I asked him about dancing. I wanted to know if he thought dancing was important for a girl to learn, the way Daddy seemed to think it was.

"I certainly don't think it's important," he told me. "Most girls at dances are so silly I can't find anything to talk to them about. I only go to parties myself because I don't wish to become a recluse."

If Wake felt tongue-tied at dances I decided I needn't bother with them, either. Because certainly Wake had more ideas to the minute than anyone I'd ever known, except my father.

Half our businessman's vacation was gone when the first storm broke. It had been building for two days, but I couldn't make Wake believe that those cloudy afternoons meant the sky would pour down buckets of water some day soon. First the clouds grew gray, then black. Daddy looked at the barometer and put the fattest chunk of pine he could find into our stove. Big drops began to spatter against the glass, hitting slowly at first, in little spurts between the gusts of wind. Then the wind came roaring down off the Clark Range and whole sheets of water pounded the windows.

We could almost see the river rising as every crack and gully on the canyon walls filled with rain and melted snow. I knew my log would soon be under water—might even be swept away. After a little the rain changed to hail—big, mountain hail, like moth balls. I thought the windowpanes would shatter.

But if the rain comes fast, it never lasts long. The minute the storm was over I went out to see how Cirque was. He looked pretty shivery, huddled against Daddy's horse in one corner of the corral. Even his beautiful tail was droopy.

"How about a good run to warm up?" I asked him.

His ears said "Let's go!"

I was wondering about Wake, too, remembering the casual way he'd anchored his pup tent to a couple of twiggy bushes. If his bedding was wet I thought it would be friendly to invite him into the cabin to dry off. I was sure Daddy wouldn't mind, though he always says we can't take in all the campers in the Sierra to dry off every time it rains.

I jumped on Cirque bareback and we galloped down the trail to where I could see Wake's tent. The granite sand was still full of puddles that splashed as we tore along, and Cirque skidded to a quick stop with his forefeet in the air. He's glorious when he does that. I wished Daddy could have seen him.

"Hi, Wake!" I shouted. "Did you get all your stuff under cover?" When nobody answered I crashed Cirque right across the dead timber to Wake's camp. He wasn't there. All his things were spread around outside the tent, soaking wet, so

I knew he must have been off taking pictures when it began to rain.

Suddenly I was frightened. I don't think I ever felt really frightened in the mountains before. Daddy never lets us get into jams, because he knows ahead of time where danger lies; but Wake was such a baby in the woods, slipping and stumbling, never paying any attention to where he was going because he was so busy thinking about his lovely pictures. I was sure he had gone to photograph the cascades, for he'd been talking about them so much, never satisfied with the shots he had already made.

My heels dug into Cirque, and he bounded straight ahead, like a deer through underbrush. I headed for my log because I was positive that was where Wake had crossed the river. The Merced had risen at least ten inches, and the current was so strong that even a champion swimmer would have been dashed over the falls. It was sweeping across the top of the log now, and I dared not try to cross on it.

Then I saw his head—the rest of him was under water. I'm never going to forget the way his eyes looked. They were wide open and glinty, like a wild animal's facing a light at night. With one hand he was clinging to a branch of driftwood that had wedged against my log; with the other, he was trying to hold his camera out of the water. He saw me, too, but I knew he couldn't hear my voice. The water was so loud it drowned the sound.

There was no time to go for Daddy. Wake was

63

on the upstream side of the log, but the driftwood
he was clinging to might come loose any minute.
Then the water would sweep him right under the
log. If that happened he wouldn't have a chance.
Not against the cascades. I thought of old Mr.
Scripps washing the whole way down to Nevada
Falls. Cirque and I were going to have to get
Wake out! There wasn't any other way. "Please
God," I prayed, "make the driftwood stick togeth-
er until we get there."

Cirque understood too, I think. He began quivering all over as I urged him right to the edge of
the river. "Come on, Cirque," I whispered, wish-
ing my bare heels were spurs. In a moment the current was swirling around his knees. He planted his
forefeet on the bottom and refused to budge.

"Cirque!" I cried. "We've got to get Wake out
of there quickly!"

He lowered his head, sniffing the roily brown
water, then looked around at me as if he were saying, "Meg, old girl, it's too much for us. The old
Merced is too strong for you and me."

A terrible gust of wind whipped the branches
of a tree against my face. I realized then exactly
what I would have to do. Without my weight
Cirque stood a chance of crossing the river. But
he would have to be driven forcibly into the water.
I leaned as far forward as I could and screamed
at Wake, "Catch Cirque's tail!" Then I stood up
on Cirque's back and grabbed the tree branch with
one hand. With one foot I whacked him across the
rump with all my might and bellowed, "Go on,

Cirque!" Startled, he lunged into the stream, while I swung over the water. It was hard getting my legs up on the branch, because it wasn't steady like the pine over the corral. But finally I made it.

Blessed Cirque. He understood. He waded out as far as he could toward Wake, and all I could do was to sit there, biting blood out of my lips. When the current took him he began to swim, struggling with all his brave stock-horse heart against the flood water. Wake had to let his camera go, but he caught Cirque's tail and the horse dragged him, slowly but surely, up on the other side.

I thought, of course, that Wake would jump on Cirque, ride to the junction bridge and back to the Ranger cabin for Daddy. But I could see that he was too exhausted to move.

Cirque stood over him, sniffing with his velvet nose. Then he pawed the ground as if he were saying, "Come on! My mistress can't hang on that branch forever." But Wake just lay there, shivering. Cirque tossed his head and whinnied—then crashed off into the underbrush alone. It's five miles to the junction bridge and five miles back on our side of the river, so I knew I'd have to hang on a good long time. But I never supposed any time would *feel* so long. I tried to settle myself more comfortably in the crotch of the tree, and watched the mad waters swirling around the trunk.

Daddy came at last. He lassoed me with a rope, then threw another rope over the branch for me to shinny down. When I felt the ground under my feet again and Daddy's arms around me, I got silly and cried. He tossed me up in back of his saddle, and all the way back to the cabin I hugged him around the waist, tight, the way I used to ride when I was a little girl. Daddy said Cirque must have galloped every inch of the way. He'd come to the corral fence lathered with sweat, in spite of the icy wind, and Daddy had known right away, when he saw him riderless, that something had happened to me.

"Get yourself warm, Meg; then put plenty of water on to heat and fill every bottle you can lay your hands on. Make a hot drink," he called back as he dashed out the door, "and warm some blankets in front of the fire."

I was so busy carrying out his instructions that it didn't seem any time before he was back with the still dripping Wake. Daddy took off Wake's clothes, bundled him into a pair of flannel pajamas and wrapped him in the warm blankets lined with bottles of hot water. In a little while he was able to sit up and take the hot drink, and by evening he was enjoying the huge meal we brought to him on a tray.

The next morning I was getting breakfast in the kitchen when Daddy came in with a load of wood. "I can't wait any longer to ask you, Dad," I said, putting down the coffee I'd been measuring. "I've got to know about it now. Are we still going to sell Cirque?"

Daddy stood stock-still. "Sell him!" he exclaimed. "What an idea! Cirque can have a golden stall and feed on star dust mixed with diamonds as far as I'm concerned. Perhaps I rushed into things a bit too fast. You seem to be working matters out pretty well in your own way. I'm sorry about the camp, but all the arrangements are made, so I'm afraid you'll have to be a good sport about it this summer."

"Oh, I will, Dad," I vowed. "And I'll promise to enjoy it, if only we don't have to sell Cirque."

He dropped the armful of wood by the stove and went back for another. Then I did the silliest thing. I was so glad inside—too glad for words, I guess. I just cried and cried.

Wake doesn't know I cried, though. He has often told me since that he thinks I was very brave about everything. I'd rather not let him know I cried, because I'd like him to go on thinking that.

If Wishes Were Horses

————◆———◆———◆———◆———

ADELE DE LEEUW

WEDGED between Uncle Joe and Aunt Emma and pressed hard against the rail, Stacy watched the sulkies wheeling swiftly around the bend and down the track. The two-wheeled spidery carts seemed to fly over the ground, the horses' hooves thundered in swift rhythm, and Stacy, leaning far out, clutched her bag of popcorn so hard that it broke and spilled.

"It's Mr. McGregor's mare," she cried, turning a radiant face to Aunt Emma. "It's Lady! She's winning! Isn't she wonderful? Isn't she beautiful?"

"Now, for goodness' sake——" In her excitement Stacy had dropped her purse, too. "Pick it up, Stacy, quick."

"Oh, Aunt Emma, not till Lady's won. . . . There. . . . There! She's past the stand. I knew she would! Oh, I wish——"

"If wishes were horses you'd have two dozen by now," Uncle Joe said tolerantly, but Aunt Emma pressed her lips together. "I never did see such a

69

one for horses. I don't know why Clara and Dan didn't bring you up like other girls."

Tears stung at Stacy's lids, and her face felt hot. The cheering of the County Fair crowd drummed in her ears, but Stacy, for a nostalgic moment, wasn't there. She was back home—on the ranch that had been a kind of heaven to her all her life until tragedy had fallen like a black cloud, obliterating everything. Mother and Daddy gone. . . . the ranch taken over by the bank, the horses sold. Midget and Pete and Saracen and Feather and Lucky Girl and her own sweet Janey. . . .

Aunt Emma and Uncle Joe had taken her in, been good to her, given her a room newly furnished just for her, tried to make her happy. But sometimes a wave of homesickness broke over her with such force that she didn't know how she could stand it. That was when she *had* to talk about horses. . . . the horses she had known and loved, the ones she was going to have when she was old enough to work and have a ranch of her own again. She could never be truly happy until she did have them. Horses were "in her blood," as Uncle Joe said. But he said it laughingly.

He didn't really understand, he or Aunt Emma. They had never known anything but this small town, the old house with its neat garden, the well-ordered, intimate life of the village. Sometimes Stacy felt that she must stifle if she stayed here much longer in this tame, hedged-about atmosphere. She would take long walks into the country, imagining herself on a horse, riding over the prairie.

70

It was on one of those walks that she had discovered Mr. McGregor's place. The Mansion, it was called. She had heard the townpeople refer to it. It had been a gloomy stone house, with porches falling into disrepair, and high grass blotting out the curving drive under the ancient elms. Then Mr. McGregor had bought it, had brought in carpenters and masons and landscape artists, turned the big barn into a marvelous stable, imported a trainer and two stable-boys, and filled the place with horses.

The trainer's name was Mike O'Neill, the people said. He was a terror. But nothing compared to old man McGregor himself. Rich as Croesus, with a shell like a walnut, and just as bitter. Why was he so bitter with all that money, and all those horses? The townspeople shook their heads. And what was Mrs. McGregor like? Some said she was little and faded; some said she was tall and sad-faced; but nobody had ever had a good look at her. Kept to herself. There was some kind of mystery at The Mansion, of that everyone was sure.

Stacy was remembering all that as she stooped to retrieve her purse. Suddenly she made up her mind. "Be back in a minute," she said breathlessly.

She darted through the leisurely throngs to the long open shed where the race-entrants were stabled. A little wizened man with leather leggings and a bright blue shirt was leading Lady up and down, cooling her before the rub-down. He was the same bow-legged little man who had ridden Lady in the sulky like one inspired. His face was weather-brown and he clamped a cold pipe between his teeth. His cap was pulled low over his shrewd blue eyes and Stacy could see a close thatch of reddish hair. He looked a little forbidding, but she did not stop.

"You're—you're Mike O'Neill, aren't you?" she asked him.

He did not stop walking. "Sure, and who else? And who may you be?"

"I'm Stacy Landis . . . I live with the Holdens. I—I saw you win the race, and it was thrilling! But I knew you'd win—because you were driving Lady. She's the most beautiful mare I've ever seen. She has everything!"

His narrowed eyes studied her. "Ye think ye know a good horse when ye see one, do ye?"

"I do know. I know horses. And I know Lady's a thoroughbred. She—she makes me think of my Janey. Only she's better. I loved Janey, but of course I know Lady's a finer mare."

He was still studying her, as if trying to make up his mind. "You're a quare one, Miss," he said.

"Would Mr. McGregor mind if I stroked her nose?"

He bridled a little at that. "Sure, and how would I know what's in that one's mind? But he's not here, and I am, and *I'm* the one that handles the horses. So stroke her nose and be quick about it."

He watched her, under his low-pulled cap; watched Lady's ears and the way she stood under Stacy's hand. "You know your horses, I'll say that,

72

Miss. You've a way with you not many has. Now where in the wide world—"

They got no further than that. Uncle Joe, red-faced and perspiring, his face creased with worry, spied her then and shouted, "Stacy! Stacy, we've been hunting the grounds over for you!"

"I'm coming to see you and Lady," Stacy managed, over her shoulder, tearing herself away. Mike said doubtfully, "I don't know about that, Miss—" but she could not be *sure* that was what he said. Uncle Joe had her by the arm, propelling her toward an even more worried Aunt Emma.

"I declare, what got into you, Stacy?"

"Oh, Aunt Emma, I'm sorry, but I had to see Lady. . . ."

"Lady?"

"Mr. McGregor's mare. She won the race, don't you remember?"

"Maybe she did. They all look alike to me."

"Uncle Joe, don't you think I could have a horse—not a wonderful thoroughbred, just a nice horse I could ride—"

Uncle Joe mumbled, "You know we haven't the room."

"We could build—"

Aunt Emma said crossly, "And what about the feed? It's hard enough making ends meet nowadays, with the added expense and all, without your talking about getting a horse. I never heard such nonsense. Come along now; my feet hurt and we still have the shopping to do."

They didn't understand what it would mean to

her. If she had a horse that she could take care of, that she could ride and talk to, it would bring the ranch close again . . . the ranch and the corral and Mother and Daddy—everything that spelled home.

In spite of her determination to visit The Mansion stables soon, it wasn't until Spring that Stacy managed it. Then her Uncle Joe gave her a bicycle. It wasn't a horse, of course . . . but it was motion —wind in her hair—trees whizzing by—cloud-racing—all the things she loved.

She left her bicycle by the side of the road near the McGregor meadows. Lady was in the field, and a dozen others, and three wobbly-legged colts keeping close to their mothers. At sight of them, she vaulted the fence—what was a fence to a Western girl?—and walked across the meadow toward the stable, stopping only to stroke Lady and to make friends with the fuzzy colts.

"Here I am," she told Mike. He looked around a bit nervously; the stable-boys stared at her in wonder.

"How—how'd you get in?" Mike asked.

She told him, and a slow, incredulous grin swept over his lean face. "Hmm, nothin' can keep *you* out, I see."

"D'you mind?" she asked anxiously.

"Not *me*," he answered, rather cryptically. She didn't want to ask him what he meant. "Now that you're here, look your fill," he said.

She wandered over the stable for an ecstatic hour. There were stalls of shining, varnished wood, with iron grill work between. A freshly scrubbed stone floor. High windows through which the spring sunlight filtered. A tack room with silver-mounted harness, glittering in the light, and cases of cups and ribbons—blue and red. Mike would stand near the door for a while, then come and tell her some interesting bit about one of the horses; how some of the prizes had been won.

"Begorry, it's a pleasure to talk to a knowin' lass! The dolts around here don't know a bit of good horseflesh when they see it, and care less. You're not from around here, I take it?"

"No," she said. "That is, I am now . . . but I was raised on a ranch." And under his sympathetic prodding she told him about the golden days when she had had Mother and Dad . . . and her own Janey.

Stacy and Mike got to be fast friends. "It's good to have somebody to talk to," he told her one day, clamping his unlit pipe between his teeth. "Them boys are no good at all, at all—their minds on nothin' but how to get out of workin'—and Himself no satisfaction eyether. As for Herself—" he gave a shrug. "She's a lady I feel sorry for, I do that."

"Why, Mike?"

He said briskly, "Sure, and I've said too much already." He let Stacy help him curry the horses; let her lead them around the turf ring. She pored over their histories with him, and helped Mike doctor them. It was always hard to tear herself away. Other duties seemed so prosaic after that.

"When may I come again?" she'd ask, and Mike would scratch his head. After long thought he would say, "Come Wednesday . . . yes, Wednesday. And mind ye be a good gurrul in the meantime."

The days varied. Sometimes he'd ask her twice in a week; sometimes ten days would go by before he'd issue an invitation. One time there was a dreadful span of fourteen endless days. She couldn't stand it. Lady was going to foal, and she had had no news.

She rode slowly past The Mansion, back and forth, back and forth. Finally, she spurted up the drive. Someone raised a window, and called to her. She had a glimpse of a sad white face. Then the window was banged down with a crash that rattled the glass, and the shade was pulled. It puzzled her, but as soon as she got to the stable she forgot about it.

Mike was in a bad humor. One of the stable-boys was sick—or so he said—and the other was a good-for-nothing. "I'd fire the both of them," he grumbled, "but boys is hard to get these days, and I'm too old to do all the work meself."

Stacy said comfortingly, "I'll help all I can, Mike. Tell me what to do."

She worked busily beside him, going from stall to stall and renewing friendships.

"Damon's restless," Mike said. "Needs a workout. Want to take him around a bit?"

"Oh, Mike!" Stacy breathed, afraid she had only dreamt it. "Oh, Mike, may I, really?"

He held his hand out to give her a leg up, but she leaped neatly onto Damon's bare back. Mike whistled appreciatively. He watched her gentling Damon, and then out into the sunshine. "You can ride, all right," he shouted to her. She laughed with joy. It was wonderful—the feel of a horse under her again, the wind in her face, the soft thud of Damon's hooves, the sense of freedom and motion.

She circled the field a dozen times; then suddenly she saw a tall, stout man bearing down upon her, cane upraised. His face was purple with rage. She drew to a halt, and he surged forward shaking the cane in her face.

"You—you—where did you come from? What are you doing on one of my horses? What does this mean? Get off at once, get off and explain yourself."

She slid to the ground. "I'm sorry, Mr. McGregor—"

"Not a word out of you!"

Mike came running up. "Mr. McGregor, sorr—"

"Nor out of you, either. Get off this place and don't you ever come here again! The brass, the nerve of you! Get off my place, I say! I've a good mind to take this cane to you!"

"Mr. McGregor, sorr—"

"And to you, too, O'Neill! Rank carelessness! So that's what goes on behind my back, when I'm away! I saw this young scalawag coming up the drive. I couldn't believe my eyes!" His face was apoplectic. "Well, what are you waiting for? Get out!"

Stacy pedaled home furiously, the blood beating angrily in her ears. The hateful old man—hateful, hateful! Aunt Emma was horrified when she heard of the incident. "Nobody can talk like that to a Holden or a Landis! Don't you ever set foot on their place again—or near it, do you hear? That's what comes of meddling in other folks' business! You and your horses!"

But Stacy couldn't forget that ride. It had brought everything back to her, stronger, more poignantly, than ever. Her days were one long homesickness now, and she didn't see how she could live through the summer. It had been such a lovely thing while it lasted.

She lay out under the apple tree, imagining it was the hayloft; she rode her bike with closed eyes, imagining she was galloping over the field on Damon or Lady. She stared up at the stars at night, saying fervently, "Star bright, star light, first star I see tonight, I wish I may—I wish I might—" And then a long sigh. It was silly to wish. Wishes like that never came true. Never. Not here, anyway.

After that the summer dragged by in an endless succession of monotonous days. The air was hot and sultry, and even swimming did not make her feel right. She rode listlessly down the long road, one day after her swim, her thoughts ranging back to the past. Almost without her volition she found herself turning off toward the McGregor place. It wouldn't hurt just to look over the fence, would it, just to look——?

Fellow was standing under a distant tree; and she could make out Hero and Ballyhoo. But the others must be in the stable. How was Lady? she wondered. And her foal? She must have foaled by this time. Stacy's eyes turned toward the stable, and her heart stopped, then thudded fearfully. There was smoke curling from the roof, and a curl of gray wafted out of one of the windows. . . . smoke on an August day.

Stacy grabbed her wet bathing suit from the bicycle basket and tied it over her nose and mouth, vaulted the fence, and sprinted across the field. The high, whinnying neighs of the frightened horses struck at her ears as she tore through the wide doors. The air was hazy with smoke and the acrid smell of it penetrated even the wet fold around her face. Where was Mike? Where were the boys? She knew what must have happened—someone had dropped a cigarette or a match in the hayloft.

Which horse first? Oh, Lady, of course, Lady and her foal. In the special box stall she found them, Lady's eyes rolling, her nostrils showing red. Stacy flung a blanket over the horse's head, spoke to her soothingly. "Come, Lady, come, Lady. . . ." with one hand guiding her, with the other leading the stumbling little colt. She pleaded and coaxed and pushed. Lady reared and balked and whinnied, but Stacy's calm, urging voice forced her forward, into the blessed air.

She tied them to the stake at the far end of the ring; otherwise, she knew, they would blindly have followed her back. Damon next. . . . a Damon wild-eyed with fear. The smoke was thicker now, her eyes smarted and she felt choked and breathless. The noise of their frightened cries made the stable clamorous. If only someone would help! She could never get them all out in time! What if some refused to come? She mustn't think of that.

One after the other, methodically. . . . "Come, Griselda . . . nice girl. . . ." "Sultan, quiet, Sultan!" One more now. . . . King, in the last stall. He reared as she entered, and tried to throw the blanket off his head. He pawed frantically and neighed in shrill hysteria. The smoke was so thick she could scarcely see him. She strained upward to reach his halter. There were voices outside. "Good glory . . . who took them out? . . . Who's in there? Stacy, Stacy, gurrul, are ye all right?"

But she could not answer. King's rearing head jerked her arm upward and she lost her balance. She fell face forward in the stall, and everything turned black.

"It's that Mike O'Neill to see you," Aunt Emma said, her back stiff with disapproval. "I said he couldn't come in, but you could talk to him out the window."

She pushed Stacy's chair close, and laid a scarf around her shoulders. Stacy laid her bandaged hands on the sill and leaned out.

Mike was holding his cap; his red thatch gleamed

in the light. "It's a wonderful gurrul ye are, Miss Stacy, a wonderful gurrul! Mr. McGregor is after wantin' to come and see you as soon as ever he can, and Herself, too."

"I'll be glad to have them," Stacy said. "Is everything all right?"

"It is that . . . in more ways than one. And I was to tell you why he was such a curmudgeon that day and chased you off. It's like his own daughter you are, and ye gave him a start. She died these twelve years ago, a fine lass about your age. He never got over it, nor Herself eyether."

So that was the mystery of The Mansion, Stacy thought. Her heart welled with pity for the McGregors.

"He was gone that day and I to fetch him with the carriage," Mike said. "So the boys went gallivantin'. If you hadn't come along, I don't like to think— Aye, it was Providence, that's what it was. And now wait a minute; I've a present from Himself."

He disappeared around the house, and Stacy could hardly contain herself. What could it possibly be? When Mike appeared again, she cried out, "Oh, Mike, not for me! Not that darling colt for *me!*"

"And who else?" he demanded. "It's Lady's own. Look at them legs, will ye, and that muzzle, and this fine back. It's many a ribbon this one will be winning!"

A colt of her own! To love and care for and talk to! It couldn't be . . . And suddenly her face fell.

No, it couldn't be. "There isn't room," she said in a whisper. "And the feed—"

"And who said anything about room and feed?" Mike asked belligerently. "You'll keep it at the stables, of course, and Himself will pay for its keep. Then when you want to ride, there'll be the stable-full to choose from . . . and this one for your very own. You're to name her. Now, what will ye be after callin' her?"

Stacy cried, "Why, Janey, of course!" And the ranch and Mother and Daddy were close again, and she was happy as she hadn't been since she had lost them.

Brown Beauty

W. T. PERSON

IF anyone had told Janice King yesterday that she would relish a breakfast consisting of crisp-fried rainbow trout, rare bacon, and light, melty pancakes, she would have laughed. But that was yesterday, and yesterday is history.

Janice discovered that trout from the creek, which was fed by melting snow, were delicious even for breakfast, and that they harmonized astonishingly well with bacon and pancakes. It is possible that the invigorating air of Colorado had much to do with Janice's sturdy appetite.

It was while she was rather eagerly baring the fifth rib of rainbow number two that she heard sounds of excitement from without. Men were yelling; a horse's hoofs were thudding fast and heavy on the hardbaked ground.

"The boys," explained Uncle Dan King, who had noted her look of wonder, "are working with P'izen again."

"What's P'izen?"

"The prettiest piece of horseflesh I've ever owned, and about the most ornery. I'll wind up by selling him to Jim Faulhaber for rodeo work. I'm afraid that's all he'll ever be good for."

"Maybe Martin will break him yet," offered Aunt Sarah.

"Martin will, if anybody can," Uncle Dan said. "But P'izen's daddy before him was a tough one. Looks like P'izen will be even worse."

"I'll go out and watch," Janice said. "I like horses."

As she went toward the corral, Janice could see the rangy P'izen going through a series of swift contortions, leaping and bucking, rearing and dancing. But Martin Branch, foreman of Long Valley, stuck on miraculously. It was a breath-taking exhibition. Janice leaned against the corral fence and watched. She could see the lithe, tanned young foreman driving cruel rowels into the horse's ribs, forcing him to further frenzy. P'izen was wild-eyed, his nostrils distended, his ears laid back. Janice could hear him grunt as he started his furious leaps and lunges. She could hear his breath whistling.

Three cow hands were standing just inside the corral gate, ready for any emergency. The rider waved to them.

They flung open the gate, and Martin Branch forced the desperate horse toward it, through it. Then they raced away. The rider was rolling sharp spurs against the horse's sleek, straining sides.

Janice watched, sensing the horse's pain . . .

and, perhaps, some of his anger. She had never seen anything quite like this before. She wondered if it was a good introduction to Long Valley.

"Mornin', miss," one of the hands greeted her, touching his wide-brimmed hat. "How'd you like that ridin'?"

"It was fine riding, but why did he keep on spurring the horse? It seemed to make him worse."

"Got to make these crazy ones know who's boss, ma'am," the grizzled, long-faced puncher told her. "P'izen'll git spurred a lot more before he'll be fit fer anything."

"How long have you been trying to break him?"

"Brought him off'n the range 'bout a month ago," the waddy said. "But he takes a lot o' breakin'. Mart'll come back 'fore long, an' that hoss'll look tame as a kitten. He'll be plum' wore out. But next time he'll be as mean as ever. Shore looks like he's one o' them crazy ones!"

Shortly after returning to the house, Janice saw Martin coming back. The horse was in a lather. He was walking now, head down, worn out, spirit gone . . . apparently.

"The hypocrite!" Uncle Dan growled. "You'd think he was ready for work . . . but give him six hours rest and he'll act crazy again!"

"I'd be crazy too," said Janice, "if somebody hurt me like that."

"P'izen is just loco," the old rancher said. "By the way, while you're here you'd better ride Trixie, the black mare."

"Thanks, I will."

Janice had arrived for a visit at the ranch the afternoon before. Long Valley was remote. There was no telephone; the lights were kerosene lamps; the water system was a well. The nearest town, Coleville, was only five miles away; the nearest neighbor, a mile and a half. Different from the Southern plantation where Janice had been reared.

That afternoon, when she went to get Trixie and go for a ride, she met Martin, who was tall, lean, and wind-bronzed. Janice thought his eyes held a hint of amusement when he said:

"Mournful tells me you thought I was pretty hard on P'izen this morning."

"I did feel sorry for the horse," she confessed. "You didn't show him much mercy."

"You can't, with horses like that. You've got to make 'em know who's boss."

"Do you handle *all* horses that way?"

Martin smiled tolerantly down at her. "Oh, I'm not mean to horses. My own sorrel follows me around like a dog when I let him. It's different when you're breaking one fresh off the range." Then: "How do you like it here?"

"Fine . . . so far. It's different."

"We don't have much company," Martin said. "I'm glad you've come . . . for Mrs. King's sake, I mean. She'll enjoy having you around. She's by herself a lot of the time, when Boss Dan's riding over the spread."

"I thought Uncle Dan was too old to do much riding."

"He is, but that doesn't stop him. He 'tended to

everything so long that he can't get out of the habit,
I reckon. Your aunt works hard, too. Both of 'em
ought to be taking it easy; they could afford to."

During the week that followed, Janice found that
everyone on the Long Valley outfit worked hard.
Martin and the others were out and gone long before she had breakfast; they came in, usually, after
dark. Uncle Dan was gone, too, most of the time.
And Aunt Sarah was constantly finding work to do,
even when the pain in her left side and arm was
bad. She complained of the pain daily.

In the afternoons, Janice saddled Trixie, a slow,
docile, paunchy black mare, and rode about the
range. Quiet, peaceful, wide horizons . . . the
great domes, the snowlaid peaks in the distance,
the purple-hazed mesas.

During that first week, Janice began trying to
make friends with the chestnut bay. At first, the
horse paid no attention as she stood outside the corral fence and talked to him. One afternoon when
she went to the corral, he was running around the
enclosure, head high, snorting, heavy mane flying.
Beauty, grace, strength, and spirit! A poem in
flesh!

What a shame that a wild, free spirit like that
must be broken and brought under the lash of man!
He should be on the open range, leader of his own
band. He was no animal to carry burdens, to come
and go at commands.

"A brown beauty!" Janice exclaimed.

She walked around the corral toward the horse,
which had stopped running and was watching her.

But as she drew near, he lunged away with a whistling snort. She followed around the fence, still talking and calling to him. But Brown Beauty was suspicious.

Martin Branch rode up then. "You'd better let that cranky horse alone, Miss Janice," he advised. "He might bite you."

"If he bit *you*," Janice said shortly, "it wouldn't hurt you any more than you've hurt him with the spur."

Martin turned a dark red. "We don't like each other very much, do we?" he asked quietly, looking steadily down at her.

"Why should we?" Janice spoke quickly. She disliked Martin Branch's air of tolerance.

The foreman nodded gravely. "Sorry," he said. Then he turned and left her there.

The next morning the riders again went to the corral, roped Brown Beauty, bridled and saddled him . . . and the fight was on. A wild, grim, desperate battle. Brown Beauty fought with all the strength of his lean, powerful body, with all the cunning of his quick, young brain. But the burden, the hated man, stuck on his back, and the rowel continued to rake his sleek side.

Again the corral gate was opened at a signal from Martin, and they sped away. When they returned thirty minutes later, Brown Beauty was lathered, walking head down, worn to a frazzle.

"I'll sell that scoundrel yet!" Uncle Dan snapped.

"But I'd give any two horses I have if he'd show some sense. What a horse he'd be!"

When Uncle Dan and the hands had gone, Janice went out to the corral. Brown Beauty was too tired now to be angry. He was at the trough, drinking. Janice reached through the fence and touched his salt-streaked side.

He flinched, moved out of reach, looking at her. Janice held out her hand. "Come and get this sugar, fellow," she begged.

Brown Beauty looked at the white stuff, took a short step forward, stopped.

Janice tossed one of the lumps onto the ground at his feet. The horse, after snorting over it investigatively, nibbled at it. Then he took the whole lump and fairly smacked over the sweetness.

"Here's some more. Come." Janice held out her hand.

Brown Beauty promptly threw precaution to the wind. He nuzzled her hand, knocking the delicious lumps onto the ground. He ate them eagerly.

When Janice returned to the corral that afternoon, Brown Beauty did not move away from the fence until she tried to pat his proud neck. When she touched him, he wheeled away from her.

But the next morning, after much persuasion and soft talking, Janice managed to make him eat from her hand. Sugar, bits of apple, carrot, grain. He was clearly suspicious, though. And when she went into the corral, he became wary and cautious again. She couldn't get near him. He trotted away from her, with loud snorts. He stopped at the far side of the enclosure and pawed angrily, shaking his head as if to warn her. His ears were laid back now, and no amount of soft-worded persuasion could re-establish his confidence right then. Recent experience had taught him a bitter lesson.

For three days thereafter, Janice returned to the corral while the others were away, and tried to make friends with Brown Beauty. It was a slow process, requiring caution and tact; but Janice was patient and gentle and kind. Confident and determined, too. If the King streak hadn't been strong in her, she would have given up in despair.

Finally, Brown Beauty accepted her inside the corral and nibbled choice morsels from her hand while she stroked his sleek neck with a heavy brush until it shone like burnished silk. She tugged at his heavy mane, scratched his velvety muzzle, the while talking reassuringly to him. That, for Janice King, was a day of rare joy.

But she knew that it was only the beginning. All along, Janice had been determined to ride Brown Beauty. Now she must get bridle and saddle on him —and with no husky cow hands to help her.

On her next visit to the corral, she carried a bridle, but made no attempt to put it on the horse. Instead, she let it hang from her shoulder, so that he could get used to the sight of it. That afternoon she tried to get the bit into Brown Beauty's mouth, but he clamped his jaws and refused to accept the crooked, tasteless thing. He wasn't ugly about it, though. Just stubborn.

Janice persisted for two days and won out. Brown Beauty took the bit—from curiosity or, perhaps, sheer weariness!—and allowed Janice to pull the head harness over his ears. Then he stood still and chewed the bit investigatingly and shook his head as if the metallic taste of it displeased him.

It was a full week after this before Janice managed to get a saddle on Brown Beauty. A week of patience and persistence called forth by more than her love for horses: she was meeting the unspoken challenge of Martin Branch! Danger aside—and there *was* an element of danger involved—it was task enough to get blanket and saddle on Brown Beauty, who shied and trembled whenever she made a motion with these hated contrivances.

Janice gradually overcame his nervousness, and after seven days of trying, she accomplished her purpose. Brown Beauty stood bridled and saddled.

Jim Faulhaber, the rodeo entrepreneur, who had heard of this fine, untamed horse of Dan King's, came out to Long Valley on a Wednesday afternoon. But there was no rider on hand, which pleased Janice. She walked to the corral with Uncle Dan and the visitor, heard them talking horses and prices. She winced when the rodeo promoter said:

"He looks like a horse I can use, all right. Mean eye."

"He's a tough one," Uncle Dan admitted regretfully. "If I had a rider here, you'd see something."

"I'll drop out again tomorrow," Mr. Faulhaber promised. "He can do his stuff for me then."

Janice was awake that night long after Uncle Dan and Aunt Sarah were asleep. She was fighting temptation. Once, shortly after the moon had risen, she slipped from bed and dressed, determined to turn Brown Beauty out of the corral. Freed, the horse might go so far away that Martin would never find him. He might escape being made into a fiend of a horse by Mr. Faulhaber, who had black, cruel eyes.

She was almost at the corral gate when a voice called, "Miss Janice."

She stopped, her heart pounding. "What?" She tried to sound brave and undisturbed. "What do you want?"

A tall figure was coming toward her. She knew it was Martin Branch. "I don't want to be meddling," he said calmly, "but if you're about to turn that horse out . . ."

"How did you know?" Janice gasped. "How . . . ?"

"I didn't know. I guessed. It's not hard to know how you feel about P'izen, and since Faulhaber was here today, I figured you might take a chance on turning the horse out tonight."

"Then you waited up to snoop!" Janice faced him in the moonlight.

"Call it snooping if you want to, but that horse is too hard to catch. I don't want to be chasing him over the range again. And besides, you're acting like a kid. P'izen belongs to Mr. King; if we can't break him, then the boss can sell him. You'd better go back to bed and forget about—"

92

"That *would* be better," Janice said coldly, anger being her only defense now, "since you're on hand to report me to Uncle Dan if I—"

But Martin broke in there: "I wish you were a man for just a few minutes," he said, his voice shaking with anger. "I'm not the snooping, tattling kind. I'm just trying to keep you from doing something you oughtn't to do."

"And what would you do if I were a man?" Janice asked sweetly. She knew that he was right, but, womanlike, she pressed the question. "Would you give me a beating?"

"I would," said Martin Branch, "unless you happened to be a better man than I am. But we're being silly, both of us! Good night." He turned abruptly and went toward the bunkhouse.

Ashamed both for what she had said and for what she had almost done, Janice stole back into the ranchhouse, and to bed. She thought she liked Martin Branch better now—although of course that didn't matter at all.

At breakfast the next morning, Janice wanted to confess to Uncle Dan that she had made friends with Brown Beauty and ask his permission to ride the horse, to prove that he wasn't bad. But she realized that such a request would only make Uncle Dan more eager to sell. He would be afraid for her. So she remained quiet.

It was during that morning, after the men had gone, that she heard Aunt Sarah call. Her voice was strange, full of suffering.

Janice ran across the hall to Aunt Sarah's room and found her sitting on the edge of the bed. Her face was white and drawn; she was breathing with painful gasps.

"What on earth?" Janice cried. "Are you . . . ?"

"It's in my chest—an awful pain—cutting off my breath."

"Lie down," Janice begged, frightened and helpless. "Maybe—"

"It hurts worse that way. I think it's—my heart. The pain comes and—goes. I—can't bear it much longer."

"I'll get the doctor," Janice told her, trying to sound confident. "I'll stop on the way to Coleville and send Mrs. Lang to stay with you until the doctor comes."

"Get Dr. Crandall," Aunt Sarah whispered. "And —hurry!"

"I'll hurry." Janice patted her shoulder. "Be brave."

She raced to the corral, whistling for Brown Beauty. He came on a high-headed trot, for she had taught him to come when she whistled like that. Janice petted him for a moment. Then she slipped the bridle on, threw the saddle into place, and drew the cinch tight.

In the saddle quickly, she patted Brown Beauty's arched neck. "Let's go, boy."

He hesitated for a bare instant, as if awaiting the cut of the rowel. The breaking process had conditioned him to expect that, to think of it as the natural accompaniment of a rider.

But this was different: This beloved one was talking gently, stroking him, tugging at his mane.

Brown Beauty set off at a brisk trot in the direction Martin had ridden him, but Janice tugged the rein gently and brought him out onto the dirt road that led to town.

The trot broke into a gallop. Janice urged him on faster, and Brown Beauty stretched out. It was swift, easy running, smooth, flowing speed. This was not mad, frenzied racing such as Martin had forced him to. This was deliberate, willing running.

After a short pause at the Lang ranch, Janice turned Brown Beauty back into the road, and they raced on.

They came to the dusty little town of Coleville and Janice reined the horse in sharply before Dr. Crandall's office.

"I've been expecting this," said the big, kindly man, reaching for his bag. "Mrs. King works too hard. I'll hurry right out."

Janice watched him leave, then started for the hitching rack.

Someone called her name.

She turned and saw Uncle Dan coming toward her. Mr. Faulhaber was with him. Their surprise at seeing P'izen bridled, saddled, and hitched was evident.

"What's that horse doing here?" Uncle Dan asked quickly. "Did *you* ride him? I've told you not to—"

"Trixie would have been too slow," Janice broke in, defending herself. "Aunt Sarah—"

"Sarah's worse?" Uncle Dan paled. "How is she? Tell me, girl."

"Dr. Crandall has just gone out. Don't think the worst, Uncle Dan. Let's hope for the best instead."

The old man nodded. "We must get out to the ranch. Come on. You'll ride in the car with me. I'll send Martin back after P'izen."

"He's not P'izen any more," Janice corrected him. "He's Brown Beauty. And I'll ride him back. You go home to Aunt Sarah—and hurry."

"Well, I reckon you can ride him home if you rode him to town," Uncle Dan reasoned, and a bit proudly. He turned to Mr. Faulhaber. "Our deal's off, Jim. The horse isn't mine any more. You see how it is."

Janice's heart leaped. Did he mean—?

"I wouldn't want him now anyway," Mr. Faulhaber said. "I hope you find Mrs. King better when you get home." He turned then and went on down the street.

"What did you mean, Uncle Dan," Janice asked quickly, "when you said that Brown Beauty wasn't yours any more?"

"I meant that he's yours, girl! You've earned him." Then the old rancher wheeled and started toward his car before Janice had time to thank him.

A mile from the ranch, Janice saw a cloud of dust sent up by a rider coming at break-neck speed. She went cold—Aunt Sarah was worse!

But when she saw Martin Branch's face, she knew that his concern and haste were not for Aunt Sarah. It pleased her somewhat to note that he looked just a little sheepish, as well as scared.

"Get off that horse this minute," he called, drawing up near her. "And don't scare me like this any more, Jan—I mean, Miss Janice."

Janice smiled at him across Brown Beauty's high head, relishing her victory. "Don't scold," she begged. "Brown Beauty's perfectly safe. How's Aunt Sarah?"

"Resting easier. Doc Crandall gave her a hypo, says she'll pull through, but that she'll have to be careful from now on. I wish you'd get off that horse."

"Oh, he's as gentle as a kitten. He prances like this because he wants to run some more. By the way, Uncle Dan made me a present of Brown Beauty a while ago."

"That so?" Martin grinned a bit sheepishly. "And now we don't have anything to fuss about."

"Oh, we'll find something," Janice predicted lightly. "Surely we'll—" But she faltered there, for the look in Martin's gray eyes had stopped her. Something new, compelling, yet unspoken. She looked down at Brown Beauty's sleek neck. "Race you home," she challenged, hoping her voice was steady. "Come—"

"Wait," Martin objected. "No hurry. Anyway, I think your horse needs to practice walking. It comes in handy sometimes."

"Does it?"

"Sure." Martin was trying to be whimsical now. "My pony's good at it. You kind of hold Brown Beauty back. He'll catch on."

As Martin pulled his pony around for the trip back, Brown Beauty shied away from the man he hated. Then he reared wildly.

"Watch him!" Martin yelled. "He's a—"

But Janice seemed to know what she was about. She had quickly brought Brown Beauty under control and was laughing at Martin Branch. "Isn't he graceful?" she asked mischievously.

"Why didn't you tell me you could ride a horse like that?" Martin asked gruffly, although pride and admiration were in his eyes. "Why didn't you—?"

"You didn't ask me," Janice reminded him.

They rode on to Long Valley, the horses walking side by side. Brown Beauty, for a beginner, was catching on very nicely.

The Horse Show

BOWEN INGRAM

THE Polkboro horse show is always held on the
first Friday evening in June, and this year Mr. Hart
took two boxes in the right center of the oval, one
for himself, Mrs. Hart and little Jennie Mai; the
other for Emme, Doby, and Red. This left a seat
conveniently vacant in each box in case Lillias
wished to visit back and forth, although there was
little doubt she'd sit most of the time by Red.

She was not to show Magic until the third ring,
and it would be late after that before she could join
them, but Emme, Red and Doby, in a frenzy of impatience, went an hour early and sat silently
through fading twilight watching occasional head-
lights cut pale swaths across the parking field.
Emme had spent half the afternoon on her nails
and chewed off all the bright new polish in the first
few minutes.

When darkness fell cars came faster and the
trickle of arriving people swelled to a river and

flowed clock-and-counter-clockwise through the stands, before settling into a lake of faces. The more restless spilled down to the rail to move ceaselessly around it until the show started and they froze against it, and all this while, in the brightly lighted ring, the chairs for the high-school band and the judges (although the judges never sat) and the wires and attachments of the public address system waited expectantly. Finally, the little gate opened at the end of the oval and eight ribbon girls in full-skirted cotton evening gowns led in the band, followed by the judges. There was a scurry for seats in the grandstand, the cold-drink boys ran down the aisles, stable boys gathered near the gate, and the eyes of the crowd focused on the ring.

The Harts arrived as the band burst out playing. Lillias' father and mother looked, to Emme, somewhat overcalm, but little Jennie Mai was her normal sharp self. They exchanged tight smiles and forgot one another. The crowd applauded and the band launched into a second piece before the announcer finished requesting it.

During this, however, Emme's dark brown gaze roamed the end of the ring where the white gate and the white paling fence stood out sharply from the black shadows. It was unbelievable how abruptly the bright light stopped at the whitewashed fence, and Emme thought at first it must be an optical illusion that she'd presently adjust to, but she never did. She never did distinguish the dark horse she sought in the darkness. Was Lillias there? Was she afraid? She had never been afraid, but there

100

is always a first time. Emme had made her own adjustment to fear, but she could not bear it for Lillias. She resumed chewing her nails. This was Lillias' first show.

Yet, why worry? Lillias was not like her; nor even like Doby, or Red, although they had not realized this until after the black filly colt was foaled and she told her father's trainer, "I'm going to show her myself, Mac; Dad says I may."

"A pretty girl never hurt a horse with the judges," Mac said.

"Am I pretty?"

"You'll do," he said briefly, "but you'll have to work."

They hadn't realized, then, what this would do to their foursome; they hadn't taken it seriously, at all. They had always talked sports together, and played tennis and swam, and Emme and Lillias hand-in-hand had cheered Red and Doby through the football season, but none of them had given horses a thought before Mr. Hart built his stables; and afterward Emme and Doby and Red had ridden only because Lillias asked them to and it was all right, occasionally, for a change. It was hard to say now, looking back, exactly when Magic began absorbing Lillias into a world they could not follow, but Emme remembered how her own enjoyment waned when Mac started riding with them and coaching Lillias, "Tighter rein, Lillias . . ." or, "Straighter, Lillias . . ." as if the others weren't there; and Lillias had followed his instructions with serious care. Emme had begun, then, to find excuses to stay at home from the riding parties, but it was not until one afternoon when Lillias forgot a swimming party that she realized with dismay that Lillias, instead of abandoning her riding, was using the same tactics to get in more of it!

She had, for a while, suffered miserably from a feeling of hurt and loss and a guilty suspicion it must be partly her own fault. She had tried desperately to love Magic as Lillias did, but in her heart she could not, and neither could she come to a closer understanding of Lillias than before. She had been too loyal to discuss it with Doby, except the day she forgot and blurted.

"She's going to the farm to ride before breakfast, now!"

"Yeah," he gazed toward the skyline abstractedly. "Who told you?"

"Red."

In a rush of returning loyalty she defended Lillias. "I guess she feels about horses like he does about football."

"Yeah."

So the three of them left it at that, their puzzled inadequacy covered by silence until their loyal interest was rewarded by cheering news. Lillias was driving toward a definite goal: to show Magic in the Polkboro ring. This had given them something definite to look forward to and encouraged them to believe it would either end there or they'd finally understand it better. They became more cheerful and talkative about it. They even kidded her occasionally, while secretly they ticked off the spring

102

days like once they had waited for Christmas, until
the real problem began to seem less one of essential
differentness than of learning to wait.

Yet, Emme thought, nobody knew how hard
waiting was until they tried it. It was a pain in your
muscles and an ache in your joints, and even now,
so near the end, it was racking her spirit. She moved
uneasily in her chair.

But, suddenly, Progress! The yearlings were entering the ring, and the crowd tautened with interest. Yearlings meant only to Emme that the
show had at last begun and she took this opportunity
to glance quickly toward the Hart box to see if
they were betraying nervousness yet, but met the
sharp eyes of little Jennie Mai and turned quickly
away. How could a sweet girl like Lillias have such
an obnoxious little sister! She took her chewed nails
from her lips and tried to make her mind a blank.
She had heard the rings always ran overtime. This
one, however, surprised her by ending on the dot,
and after a five minute pause (it seemed an hour)
the second ring was called. She sat straighter.

This was the pony ring. Kids stood up in their
seats and shrieked for their favorites, and relatives
of the youthful riders shamelessly charged the rails
and dislodged astonished railbirds the better to see
their darlings while the sentimental judges let the
ring go over time and the little rocking horses
bobbed endlessly around and around. Emme
stopped watching and stared at the railing of her
box until the last tail whisked through the gate and
Doby muttered, "Only five minutes more!" Then

she shook with a chill in spite of the hot June night and fixed her gaze, with rigid intensity, on the gate.

And the crowd, too, having got the ponies safely out of the way, settled down to serious business. The cold-drink boys did a rushing trade, the judges looked serious, the announcer drank water and mopped his brow. When he called the ring loudly, the band broke forth and every eye in the stands joined Emme's vigil at the gate. Now! said the eyes.

A tall head entered the circle of light and her heart flopped once, like a fish in a pond. Then a shining neck, with full fall of mane . . . but this is not Magic, Emme! Start breathing. This is a roan!

Ah, but he's beautiful! See how confidently he steps! And his rider knows what she's doing. This must be the Cookeville horse; watch out for him, Mac had said, he'll be tough to beat. Now another, and another; Lincoln County and Harlinsdale and Rutherford and Maury . . . each stepping imperiously toward the rail and the brief bursts of partisan applause. Now there are five, seven, nine . . . the program says ten. Ten is a large ring. Nine are in and the gate still open (after five minutes the gate will be closed said the program) but Lillias has not come.

The band played. Horses circled. The emerald oval and the white, white fence and the lights and judges waited, but she did not come. Emme's heart no longer flopped. It was curled up inside her, playing dead. Then, suddenly, it beat so loud she could hear it. Through the montage of darkness above the gate the shining head of Magic emerged and behind it, without body, floated the pale oval of Lillias' face.

For a moment Emme had the wild fantasy that her imagination had created it. Then the whole of girl and horse moved into the light and she saw Magic's neck was arched high, and Magic's hooves were lifted and put down fastidiously, as if Magic would like very much to see where her feet were being set were she not Midnight Magic, daughter of Magic Star and Allen's Midnight, blue-blooded and satin-black and too proud to lower her head. Emme saw Lillias speak to her. Lillias looked very tiny and all one with her blackness except for the pale gold hair beneath her derby and the small wedge of white stock and the white intentness of her face. She leaned forward, a little, when she spoke to Magic. And that was the moment it happened; the simple, complex thing.

A small garden toad came through the white palings, stopped; blinked; hopped uncertainly sidewise, then made a desperate blind leap straight at Magic's feet. Magic shied and Lillias went off in a soundless arc, landing flung-out as a tiny black rag doll on the emerald grass. The band broke off with a ragged screech. Grant, Magic's Negro groom, jumped the fence and ran toward her, but Lillias leapt up alone and caught Magic's rein with her left hand. In the ensuing violent silence girl and horse eyed one another. Magic, trembling, began inching backward, tossing her head.

Grant had stopped when Lillias leapt up, but now he began coming slowly on. His frightened attempt to look calm was ludicrous, yet nobody laughed. Magic lifted her forefeet lightly in the air at sight of him and her nostrils flared. Instantly he froze. The horses in the ring had slowed, and stopped. The watchers in the stands were still. The three judges stood as they had turned, caught in awkward immobility like candid snapshots in an album. Only Magic and Lillias were in motion. Magic trembled and inched backward and Lillias stood firm; slowly, firmly pulling down her head with her left hand. For a moment girl and horse came almost eye-to-eye; then lightning flashed from Lillias' right side and over the startled oval, the tense stands, the parking field to the dim sky went a loud unmistakable *konk!* Lillias had struck Magic with the loaded end of her crop!

Instantly Magic stopped trembling. Lillias bunched the reins, Grant cupped his hand, and she was up. Magic moved slowly, surely forward. Grant mopped his shining dark brow and went through the gate. The band burst forth, horses started circling again, the crowd exhaled one long breath, like a sigh, and it was over as if it had never been.

Perhaps it hadn't, Emme thought. Perhaps she had imagined it. But could you imagine a *konk* that still seemed to echo beside your ear? Yet, how could it be real that Lillias, who loved Magic better than . . . well, the whole world, perhaps . . . had struck Magic before all their eyes then calmly mounted and brought her into the ring? Smooth as silk Magic came, angling toward the rail where plops of applause began bursting like firecrackers in her face, although she seemed not to care. Lillias seemed unaware, too. They went past the Hart box, where Mr. Hart half rose and little Jennie Mai squealed; past Red and Doby and Emme, strained forward and close enough to reach out and touch them, with never a flicker or change in expression; on and on around the ring oblivious of the whole world but themselves.

How can she do it? Emme wondered. I could not! I could have hit Magic or I could have showed Magic, but I could not have hit Magic then brought her in!

She looked at Red. His flaming crest had crossed every mid-state goal line and he had left the print of his handsome face in the gridiron mud. His blue eyes were almost black as they watched Lillias, and his face was white and strained. Could he have done it? Red?

She looked at Doby. He was the quiet one who followed Red. He was leaning a little forward, his dark hair roughed by fingers hastily plowed through it, but his grey eyes were blazing back of a thin attempt to look casual. She cried, "Doby!" and he gave her a fleeting smile and the light died out, but she was shaken. Could he? Doby?

When she turned back to the ring again the slow-walk was over and the horses circling in the easy fast-walk for which they were bred. Generations of their forefathers had carried the master over his plantation while proud racehorses watched coldly from bluegrass pastures. They had not then been luxuries, like the racehorses, the carriage horses, the five-gaited aristocrats. Now plantations used sixty horses under one hood and the breed would have vanished if they had not been discovered by a new world of pleasure-riders and given a new name, walking-horses.

They had three gaits. A walk that was called a slow-walk, and a walk of easy motion and moderate speed called a fast-walk; and a canter. They were now fast-walking, but it was almost time for the canter and they knew it, and the knowledge did them no good. This was the time they broke the gait. This was the test. Magic had done well so far, but the shock of the crop had worn off and her blood was seething again. Muscles twitched beneath her glossy coat and her eyes rolled. Would she break? The judges watched her closely. Here a horse broke, quickly retrieved; there another— but Magic did not break. Tension seized the crowd; tension filled the ring. It was past time to call the canter but the judges still watched Magic. Sweat stains broke the patina of her shining coat and still she went on and on around the ring. It was cruel but when it ended Magic still held the gait.

"Canter!"

All ten horses went into the beautiful gait, and the judges relaxed and walked about while the crowd sat back and rested its hands idly in its lap. Round and round went the horses, nostrils dilated, manes rippling, tails flowing, riders leaning forward and inward, jockeying for openings ahead. Round and round came the thud of hooves and the gleaming bodies, so close that Emme heard the whistle of Magic's breath. Round and round in the race that is not a race but a test of control, where a horse must master himself, not another horse. Sporadic applause began, then settled into steady thunder punctuated with whistles and yells; and its volume was heaviest wherever Lillias went.

It was her crowd, now; no doubt about it. "The favorite," Emme whispered, awed. But Mac had warned "the favorite doesn't always win," and she said to herself, "I must not count on it. Whatever happens, win or lose, I must not care." And she thought, "No matter how it is afterward, I must not care. She is different from us, she is wonderful, we must not care."

The crowd had gone wild in a steady roar. The announcer bent into the microphone and moved his lips, but the noise defeated him. He tried twice, then walked into the ring with his hands held high and behind him the judges held up their hands until quiet fell on the crowd. Then he called the line-up in a calm voice. "Bring your horses in. Line up!" The horses slowed, reluctantly, and began stepping high and daintily into place before the judges. The judges went to the head of the line and began their own slow walk.

They took more than usual time on each horse. Each stop down the line was greeted with fresh spurts of applause and one horse broke nervously and circled away, and back. Now they had come to Magic, and whistles pierced the applause. Now they were past, but their faces told nothing. Magic was beautiful. Was that what they wanted? What did they want, anyway, in a horse? Sometimes they made strange choices. The favorite did not always win.

The ribbon girl waited, tired of trying to look un-tired. She flicked an unseen insect from her organdy frock. The announcer fanned his face with a pro-gram, while noise slowly died out of the crowd again. Then, suddenly, things moved fast. The judges beckoned; the ribbon girl took the ribbons toward the line, toward Magic. She held up her hand; Lillias bent . . . ah, the blue! The crowd and the band burst simultaneously into cacophony. Lillias pulled away, circled the ring once with the blue fluttering from between her teeth, and after her came the red ribbon, and the white, and the fol-lowing stream of horseflesh; and it was over. There had been nothing of change in Lillias' face as she flashed by, for Emme had especially watched her face.

Doby and Red solemnly shook hands then turned to Emme, but she was hunched down in her seat still staring at the gate, so they began loudly cover-ing her emotion, "Boy! Wasn't that sump'n!" and, "I'll say!" In the next box big Jennie Mai sank back in her chair, trembling, and little Jennie Mai for once looked impressed, but Mr. Hart jumped up and began shaking hands with the friends surging down to congratulate him; beckoning the cold drink boys over and handing out bottles with aban-don. "That horse'll take the Whiteman cup some day," Emme heard. "You'll bring it to Polkboro, Baxter!"

"My girl'll bring it," he said proudly. This wasn't in the best tradition but Emme thought the remaining occupants of his two boxes were dead-pan enough to balance him off. She was exhausted. "I'll never understand horses," she thought, "or judges; but it doesn't matter." Then she had a flash of insight. "I'll never understand Lillias, either, but she's wonderful and that's enough."

The racket of the band snapped her sharply back to the show. The carriage ring was entering, the four tiny wheels spinning forward so fast they seemed to reverse and spin backward, and perhaps they had. Why not? It would be as real as other things she'd seen. The crowd greeted them with as much enthusiasm as if they hadn't just worn out their hands on Lillias, as if they'd never clapped for ponies, or yearlings; as if they'd never get enough. But for her the show was over, with an aftermath of dulled perception. Why didn't Lillias come?

It was next to the last ring before she came, and the jumpers were leaving. She had changed to a gingham suit and her hair was brushed sleekly back in the way she wore it to school, but the blue fluttered from her lapel. She paused beside her father and he gazed lovingly at his first blue, then she slipped in the box beside Red.

"I stayed awhile with Magic," she said. Red just looked at her, saying nothing. "The music scared her before we went in. We slipped on that. We should have tried her before with a band." She laid her hand lightly on Red's arm and looked past him to Doby, then Emme. And Emme heard her own voice, too loud and high.

"Oh, Lillias! I'm so glad you're back!"

People turned to look, and grin; thinking she meant back from the ring. Red and Doby shouted with laughter. But Lillias smiled into her eyes serenely, understanding. She was still Lillias, and she was back. That wonderful stranger with the courage to strike Magic, her beloved, rather than let her disgrace her blood and panic the other horses had vanished in the shadow beyond the ring and this girl in gingham had come back saying, "We slipped on that," with her hand on Red's arm. Why did I think it would be different, Emme wondered. What a dunce I am! She joined the laughter and excited chatter. She cheered for the favorite in the grand champion ring and cried "No!" when the judges passed him up. She had never had so much fun.

At the end of the show, while Lillias was being congratulated by friends and strangers, Emme and Doby and Red stood in a group apart, but afterward they walked toward the parking field with her in a close line. The Harts had gone and left Mac to drive them in and they stood by the car, the last in the field, while he finished seeing about Magic. With all their wisdom, they were still too young for a driver's license, and they must wait for Mac.

The late half-moon had risen. It illumined the field with a gentle clarity that failed to dim the stars. A light breeze had sprung up. It brushed across their faces, and the cut grass in the field yielded a fragrance like new hay. Suddenly Red kissed Lillias. They had all been looking up idly at the stars, he was standing beside her; he bent and kissed her. It was no snatched kiss, he did not hurry, and she did not move although the black of her pupils widened and spread over her startled eyes, making two black mirrors in which the stars were reflected, tiny and clear. He had never kissed her before, and she had wondered why. Doby had kissed Emme, and Emme wondered, too.

"I think it's because he has such high ideals," Lillias had decided. "I think he isn't sure yet he's going to marry me. I think he will, when he is."

Emme agreed. There was not much she could offer in experience based on Doby's kiss, except he'd kissed her. She was not at all sure it meant he knew he'd marry her, in fact she was pretty sure the idea had never occurred to him; so she was glad of the delicate etiquette which prevented discussing it in detail while Lillias was still unkissed. Now, she saw with relief, there would still be little to discuss. Red's kiss had been about like Doby's, although Doby had kissed her on the porch where it was dark so there was no way of knowing whether or not she'd got stars in her eyes except when she went upstairs and looked in the mirror they were very bright. Red released Lillias, but she did not move. She was looking at his face; she did not even notice a flutter of shadow from her shoulder to the ground.

After a small wait, Emme stooped and picked it up.

"Your blue, Lillias!"

"Oh, that!" Her laugh was clear and gay. "Whatever will I do with it? Here, keep it for me, Red!"

She stuffed it gaily in his pocket as Mac came toward them across the field.

The Winning of Dark Boy

JOSEPHINE NOYES FELTS

"I DON'T believe it. I just don't believe it!" whispered Ginger Grey to herself as she watched Dark Boy, the beautiful black steeplechaser, going round and round on the longe, the training rope to which he was tethered in the O'Malleys' yard. She was stroking him with her eyes, loving every curve, every flowing muscle of his slender, shining body.

But the voice of Tim O'Malley, Dark Boy's owner, still echoed in her ears. "You're a brave little horsewoman, Ginger, but Dark Boy would kill you. I am getting rid of him next week. He's thrown three experienced men and run away twice since I've had him. You are not to get on him!"

Ginger wiped a rebellious tear from her cheek, looking quickly around to make sure that neither ten-year-old Tommy nor the two younger children had seen her. She was alone at the O'Malley farm, several miles away from home, looking after the O'Malley children for the day while their father

115

and mother were in town. Why couldn't she have had the exercising and training of this glorious horse! Her heart ached doubly, for she longed to ride him next week in the horse show at Pembroke.

Ginger glanced now at the two little girls playing in the yard. They needed their noses wiped. She took care of this, patted them gently, and went back to where Dark Boy was loafing at the end of the longe. He didn't seem to mind the light saddle she had put on him. The reins of the bridle trailed the ground. She must go soon and take it off. He'd had a good workout today, she thought with satisfaction. Exercise was what he needed. And now with nobody riding him . . .

She shivered suddenly and noticed how much colder it had turned. A great bank of black clouds had mounted up over the woods behind the meadow. She studied the clouds anxiously. Bad storms sometimes rose quickly out of that corner of the sky. The air seemed abnormally still and there was a weird copper light spreading from the west.

If it was going to storm she'd better get the children in the house, put Dark Boy in the barn, and find Tommy. Here came Tommy now, dirty, tousled, torn pants legs flapping as he walked.

"Barbed wire," he explained cheerfully, pointing to his pants. "Zigafoos has fenced his fields with it!"

A sharp gust of wind rounded the house. Tommy flapped in it like a scarecrow. A shutter on the house banged sharply; the barn door creaked shrilly as it slammed. Dark Boy reared and thudded to the ground.

116

"Look!" yelled Tommy suddenly. "What a close funny cloud!"

A thin spiral of smoke was rising from behind O'Malley's barn. Ginger's heart froze within her. Fire! She raced around the barn. Then she saw with horror that the lower part of that side was burning. The wind must have blown a spark from a smoldering trash pile. Already the blaze was too much for anything she and Tommy could do. She'd have to get help at once!

As she tore back toward the house, pictures flashed through her mind. The big red fire truck was in the village six miles down the road. There were no phones. Any cars in the scattered neighborhood would be down in the valley with the men who used them to get to work at the porcelain factory. She'd have to get to the village and give the fire alarm herself immediately. Perhaps on Dark Boy . . .

She dashed over to him and caught his bridle. He tossed his head and sidled away from her, prancing with excitement. As she talked quietly to him, with swift fingers she loosened the longe, letting it fall to the ground. She felt sure that she could guide him if only she could get on him and stay on him when he bolted. She thrust her hand deep in her pocket and brought out two of the sugar lumps she had been saving for him.

"Sugar for a good boy," she panted and reached up to his muzzle. Dark Boy lipped the sugar swiftly, his ears forward.

With a flying leap Ginger was up, had swung

117

her right leg over him, and slipped her right foot in the stirrup. She sat lightly forward as jockeys do. Would he resent her? Throw her off? Or could she stick?

Indignant, Dark Boy danced a wide circle of astonishment. The wind was whistling furiously now around the house, bending the trees. Ginger held the reins firmly and drew Dark Boy to a prancing halt. Then suddenly he reared. She clung with her lithe brown knees and held him tight. Precious minutes were flying. She thought of the bright tongues of flame licking up the side of the barn.

"Tommy! Take care of the children!" she shouted over her shoulder as Dark Boy angrily seized the bit between his teeth and whirled away. "I'll get help!"

Ginger's light figure in a red blob of sweater flashed down the road through the twisting trees. Fast as Dark Boy's bright hooves beat a swift rhythm on the hard clay road, Ginger's thoughts raced ahead. She glanced at her watch. By the road it was six miles to the town. At Dark Boy's throbbing gallop they might make it in fifteen minutes. By the time the fire department got back it might well be much too late.

There was a crash like thunder off in the woods to her left as the first dead tree blew down. Dark Boy shied violently, almost throwing her headlong, but she bent lower over his neck and clung. Suddenly her heart stiffened with dread. What had she done! She'd been wrong to leave the children.

118

Suppose Tommy took them into the house, and the house caught fire from the barn! She hadn't thought of the wind and the house. She'd only thought of saving the barn!

Desperately she pulled at Dark Boy's mouth. But he was going at a full runaway gallop, the bit between his teeth. Stop now? Go back? No!

There was one way that she might save precious seconds: take him across the fields, the short cut, the way the children went to school. That way it was only two miles! There were fences between the fields, but Dark Boy was a steeplechaser and trained to jump. She'd have to take a chance on jumping him now. They thundered toward the cut-off.

Peering ahead for fallen trees as the branches groaned and creaked above her, she guided him into the little lane that ran straight into a field where the main road turned sharply. Now he was responding to her touch, his great muscles flowing under his glossy coat like smoothly running water. She held him straight toward the stile at the far end of the field. Here was the place to take their first jump. Would he shy before it and make them lose the moments they were saving? Or would he take it smoothly?

She leaned anxiously forward and patted Dark Boy's silky neck. "Straight into it, beautiful! Come on, Boy!"

Dark Boy laid back an ear as he listened. A few yards ahead of the stile she tightened the reins, lifted his head, and rose lightly in the stirrups. Dark

Boy stretched out his neck, left the ground almost like a bird, she thought. His bright hooves cleared the stile.

"Wonderful, beautiful Boy!" Ginger cried as they thudded on.

Now to the second fence! Over it they went, smooth as silk. Her heart lifted.

Down below them in the valley the little town of Honeybrook flashed in and out of sight behind the tortured trees. She thought briefly of the steep bank from the lower field onto the road below. What would Dark Boy do there? Would he go to pieces and roll as horses did sometimes to get down steep banks? Or could she trust him, count on his good sense, hold him firmly while he put his feet together and slid with her safely to within reach of the fire alarm?

They were headed now across a rounded field. Dark Boy lengthened his glistening neck, stretched his legs in a high gallop. Just then, irrelevantly, Tommy flashed into Ginger's mind, his torn pants leg flapping in the wind. "Barbed wire! Oh, Dark Boy!"

Here was a danger she had not considered, a danger that stretched straight across their path, one she could not avoid! The lower end of Zigafoos' field, the one they were crossing now at such headlong speed, was fenced with it. Dark Boy couldn't possibly see it! This time she would be helpless to lift him to the jump. He'd tear into it, and at this pace he would be killed. She would never give her warning. Her heart beating wildly, she pulled the reins up to her chest.

"This way, Boy!" turning his head.

He curved smoothly. There weren't two of them now; horse and rider were one. They made the wide circle of the field. First at a gallop, then dropping to a canter and a walk. She stopped him just in time. He was quivering, shaking his head, only a few feet from the nearly invisible, vicious wire. As she slid to her feet the wind threw her against him.

"Here, Boy, come on," she urged breathlessly. Dark Boy, still trembling, followed her. She skinned out of her sweater and whipped its brilliant red over the barbed wire, flagging it for him. "There it is, Boy, now we can see it!"

Dark Boy was breathing heavily. Without protest this time, he let her mount. She dug her heels into his flanks and put him back into a gallop for the jump. Amid a thunder of hooves she took him straight for the crimson marker. Dark Boy lifted his feet almost daintily, stretched out his head, and they were clear!

He galloped now across the sloping field. "Good Boy, good Boy!" she choked, patting his foaming withers as he stretched out on the last lap of their race against fire and time.

The wind was still sharp in her face, but the terrifying black clouds had veered to the south, traveling swiftly down the Delaware valley. She could see distinctly the spire of the old church rising above the near grove of trees. How far beneath them it still seemed! That last fifty feet of the trail they would have to slide.

"Come on!" she urged, holding the reins firmly, digging her heels into his flanks to get one last burst of speed from his powerful frame. They flew along the ledge. Ahead in the clearing she could see the long bank that dropped to the road leading into the town. Just under top runaway speed but breathing hard, Dark Boy showed that the race was telling on him. With gradual pressure she began to pull him in.

"Slow, Boy, slow," she soothed. "You're doing fine! Don't overshoot the mark. Here we are, old fellow. Slide!"

His ears forward, his head dipped, looking down, quivering in every inch of his spent flanks, Dark Boy responded to the pressure of her knees and hands. Putting his four feet together, he half slid, half staggered down the bank and came to a quivering stop on the empty village street not ten feet from the great iron ring that gave the fire alarm. He was dripping and covered with foam.

As Ginger's hand rose and fell with the big iron clapper, the clang of the fire alarm echoed, and people ran to their doors. The alarm boomed through the little covered bridge up to Smith's machine shop. The men working there heard it and, dropping their tools, came running, not bothering to take off their aprons. It rang out across Mrs. Harnish's garden. Mr. Harnish and the oldest Harnish boy heard it and vaulted lightly over the fence, then ran, pulling on their coats.

While the big red engine roared out of the Holms' garage and backed up toward the canal bridge to get under way, Ginger called out the location of the fire. She fastened Dark Boy securely to a fence and climbed into the fire truck. They roared away up the hill.

Ginger looked at her watch again. In just eight minutes she and Dark Boy had made their race through the storm. It seemed eight hours! A few more minutes would tell whether or not they had won.

"Please, God," Ginger whispered, "take care of Tommy and the girls!"

They slowed briefly at Erwin's corner to pick up two more volunteers, then sent the big red truck throbbing up Turtle Hill. Tears trickled down between Ginger's fingers. Ned Holm threw an arm gently around her shoulders.

"Good girl!" he said smiling at her reassuringly. "We go the hill up! We get there in time!"

Ginger shook the tears from her eyes and thanked him with a smile. But at the wheel Rudi set his lips in a grim line as he gave the truck all the power she had and sent her rocking over the rough road. Her siren screamed fatefully across the valley. A barn can burn in little time and catch a house, too, if the wind is right, and this wind was right!

"How'd you come?" he growled.

"Across the fields—on Dark Boy."

"Dark Boy!" Rudi's eyes narrowed and he held them fixed to the road as he steered.

123

Ned Holm gasped. "You mean that steeple-chaser nobody can stay on?"

"I stayed on!"

They rounded the turn at the top of the hill. Now they could see the great black cloud of smoke whirling angrily over the O'Malleys' trees. As they came to a throbbing stop in the O'Malleys' yard and the men set up the pump at the well, a corner of the house burst into flames. Five minutes more and . . . !

Tommy ran panic stricken toward them. The barn was blazing fiercely now and in a little while all that would be left of it would be the beautiful Pennsylvania Dutch stone work. A stream of water played over the house. Sparks were falling thick and fast but the stream was soaking the shingles.

Ginger caught Tommy in her arms. "Where are the kids?" she shouted.

"In—in the house. I carried them up and then put the fence at the stairs. They don't like it much!"

Ned Holm ran with Ginger up the steep, narrow stairs and helped her carry out the squirming, indignant children.

That night when the fire was out and the big O'Malleys were home, the little O'Malleys safely in bed, Ginger at home told her mother all about the day. She was a little relieved that nobody scolded her about riding Dark Boy. Her mother just cried a little and hugged her.

Next morning they saw Tim O'Malley riding Dark Boy up the Greys' lane. Ginger raced out to meet him. Tim swung down and led the black horse up to Ginger.

"Here's your horse," he said simply. "You've won him!"

Ginger stared at him speechless.

Tim went on. "I want you to ride Dark Boy next week in the Pembroke show. And I expect you to win!"

"We'll try, sir," said Ginger.

On the Hoof

ANN SPENCE WARNER

KAY BENNING always groomed Red Wing last, just as she saved until last her favorite piece of candy. Then she could give extra brushes to the sorrel mare's glinting tawny mane and tail. Kay had little time to ride Red Wing these days, but just to work around her was a joy.

A final brisk rub along the haunches—ah, now the gleaming coat was perfect. But those thin ribs! Faster than she could build up the mare, Mr. Todman wore her down. If he rode her a few more times as he had last week, Red Wing was going to be in really bad shape.

Clarke Grant's bicycle bell sounded from down the driveway. Kay's thin face lighted. Clarke, a schoolmate of hers in wintertime, lived on the outskirts of the city, near the road to the Benning place, and came to the stables often. Here was someone with whom she could talk over her troubles. Her mother understood horses so little that it was no comfort taking business problems to her. Clarke got the point.

"How's the big boss?" he greeted her.

"Oh, Clarke! We hear Dad won't be back for weeks yet. And I simply don't know what to do until he gets back."

"Same as you've been doing." He was always quick with encouragement. "Everything looks ship-shape to me."

"It's Red Wing."

"So Mr. Todman's back again."

"I'll say. And a man like him—how can I refuse him the horse he wants? Especially when we still owe him on the last feed bill. Clarke!" She grabbed his arm desperately. "That's his coupe coming up the road now. Look—Red Wing in plain sight. No chance of getting her out of his way."

"Tell him she's promised."

"He'll see no one comes for her. Anyhow, you know lying never gets you anywhere. And I can't have trouble with him while Dad's away—sick, and worried to death with me in charge when he feels I'm just a kid."

There had been no one else her father could call upon. Her mother—well, as Mr. Benning always said with a laugh, you could take some people out of the city but you never took the city out of them. Mrs. Benning was afraid of horses and understood nothing about the livery business.

"Oh, I wish I knew what Dad would do if he were here," Kay whispered. Mr. Todman was step-ping out of his coupe in riding togs. "He always hated to let Mr. Todman have Red Wing but he felt he had to do it. Still, Red never used to get so completely upset as she has lately. I just can't understand it."

Mr. Todman would bring the sensitive mare in wet, nervous, completely unstrung. He always rode too hard, handled a horse too roughly; yet that should not account for the quivering nerves that lately could not be quieted for hours, for days. After he left, Kay would walk Red Wing up and down, cool her and rub her. But still there were the shuddering twitches.

"Ha! I see you have my horse for me," he declared in his heavy jovial voice. "Give me the same saddle I had the last time I rode."

There was nothing Kay could do except get the mare ready.

"Come over here," Clarke called to her. "I've got something to show you."

"Be with you in a minute," Kay answered as she watched Mr. Todman start off.

Clarke had a wounded pheasant, holding it covered up in the basket on the handlebars.

"I saw him in the field as I rode by—hopping and flopping."

Kay's gentle exploring fingers quickly located a place where a shot had gone into its body. "Oh, if only that dumb hunter could aim straight! It's bad enough having him break the law protecting pheasants. But he doesn't even kill them. His aim . . . " The grinding of her teeth was more expressive than words. "I found two last week. Feel how

129

thin this bird is. I'll bet it was shot at the same time and it's been suffering ever since."

Days of suffering had so weakened and bewildered the wild creature that it welcomed the shelter of her arms. Kay's tender fingers gently caressed the red feathers about its bright eyes, the dark head set off with the showy white collar, and the body plumage glinting with brilliant greens, reds, saffrons, and blends of other rich hues.

"I'd love to get a picture of that bird," Clarke declared, "but I left my camera at home. It wouldn't take me long to get it, though."

They both saw the flat tire at the same moment. "Aw, heck!"

"This bird's drooping so the picture wouldn't be much anyhow," Kay offered cheerfully.

"You never think any picture is much," Clarke grumbled.

It was true that Kay found it hard to share his absorbed enthusiasm for photography. She saw no sense in poking around in a stuffy, spookily-lit room when she could be riding in the sunshine!

"Who do you suppose can be doing the shooting?" Clarke wondered. "The law's so strict."

Suddenly Kay's eyes narrowed. Red Wing's quivering nerves. And how the mare hated a gun! Kay had found the wounded bird in the pasture the day after Mr. Todman last took Red Wing out.

"Mr. Todman!" she exclaimed. "I noticed today how awkwardly he got into his saddle. Do you suppose he could have had a gun concealed under his coat and breeches?"

Clarke's face reflected the excitement in hers. "He'd be the sort. Say, if we could just catch him!"

"Lot of good that would do!" Kay replied bitterly. "Who'd believe our word against his? The highly respectable Mr. Todman!"

"They would if . . ." He broke off, scowling in the direction of his flat tire. "That pesky tire! If it didn't take so doggone long to patch it!"

"Gabbing and fussing won't hurry it up." Kay had missed the connection in his mind. She finished with a comradely grin. "Better get busy."

"I'm going for a ride first," Clarke announced abruptly. "Mind if I take Dundy?"

"He isn't spoken for this afternoon," Kay said slowly. Dundy was a wise, reliable horse and the temptation was to send him out too often. Whatever else, Kay did not want Dundy out of condition. Still, Clarke handled a horse right. And it was late for more calls. "All right. Take him."

Kay was so intent on her painstaking care of the wounded pheasant that she did not even notice in which direction Clarke rode away. She bedded the bird down in a comfortable straw nest in an empty grain room, hopeful that it might be saved.

Would Mr. Todman never get back? Heartsick with concern, Kay had to keep her hands occupied. Jack, a neighborhood boy who helped her with the heavy work, had appeared to begin his evening chores. She got him to lend a hand in yanking off Clarke's flat tire so she could patch the damaged tube. Mr. Todman had been out more than his customary two hours. Poor, poor Red Wing!

Too bad this tire had had to be flat when Clarke wanted his camera.

Ah, there at last was Red Wing. Kay held her breath as the mare came nearer. Sweat streaks all over her. Drying foam on her bit, her nostrils, her neck, her flanks. That twitch of her drooping head.

Kay's eyes avoided Mr. Todman's face. She answered his remarks briefly, struggling to control the anger surging through her. Now, now while it meant so much to avoid trouble with her father away, she must not let her temper get uppermost. She must not say things to anger him.

She watched the man closely. If he had carried a gun earlier, it was not in evidence now. She had to let him inspect the wounded pheasant and not tear into him for the brute, the pheasant killer she suspected him to be. She had to stand debating with him who the hunter might be. He even suggested Clarke.

Oh, no, Kay disagreed; not possibly. Would the man ever go? At last he started for his car, but her relief was short. For as he left, he informed her that he was taking his vacation at home. He would be out the following afternoon, every afternoon that week.

By the time his car had circled the driveway, Kay's hands were trembling so that she was frightening Red Wing more than she was soothing her. If she could only take a ride on the mare, together they could outrun the horror of that man. They could lose themselves in the joy of the swift trot, the rhythm, the music of its thudding beat. But

Red Wing was too tired. She must be quieted, blanketed, and put in her box stall to rest; Kay's brush stroke widened in a soothing measure.

Still the mare quivered under her touch. Another ride tomorrow with Mr. Todman! Red Wing could never stand it. Something must be done to prevent it. But what?

Clarke was coming up the lane. She stared incredulously at the horse and the rider. Dundy was limping. His body was streaked with sweat. He was in the worst shape any horse had been returned in years. And Clarke—Clarke!—was the offender. And he wasn't even saying he was sorry. He swung off the horse and dropped the reins.

"Mind putting Dundy up for me? I've got to get home in a hurry."

Kay could not speak. For Clarke to do this to Dundy! Mr. Todman had suspected him of doing the shooting. Could he have done that, too? But Clarke was a good shot. He—oh, Clarke wouldn't . . . Yet old Dundy here . . .

"Say, you fixed the tire!" Clarke's voice was excited, happy. "Atta girl!"

Kay touched Dundy. Yes, his coat was caked, growing chilly now. He lifted one hoof, as if his leg ached. Kay saw that the shoe was worn off half an inch in front. On top of everything, Clarke had been riding him on a hard road. Clarke!

"You were swell to fix it," Clarke's pleased voice was telling her. "Now I can get away without losing a sec."

A hard road! If he had cut across Fletcher's pasture and then taken two miles of the highway, he would have been home.

"Clarke," she called after him, "did you ride after your camera?"

"How did you know? I didn't want to get your hopes up till I found out if I did get a picture to show up Mr. Todman."

Kay ran toward him. "Did you snap him?"

"Have to let you know later," Clarke called as he left.

Kay hurried back to Dundy. She must rub him down, put on poultices. Her mind raced her hands. Suppose Clarke had a picture of Mr. Todman firing a gun. What would that prove? It would be too wild to hope that the same picture could show the pheasant, too. Clarke in his excitement had never stopped to think.

But suppose she got evidence to support the picture. Suppose she found traces of the slain bird. Only where would she look? It would soon be dark. By the time Clarke reached home so she could ask him over the telephone it would be too late to start.

Her eyes fastened on the leg she was beginning to sponge. Dundy's hoofs had given her one clue. Carefully she studied the fetlock. That blackish-red clay could be found only in Smith's creek pasture. And the bridle path passed it.

If she found evidence of freshly killed pheasants and if the picture turned out, they would have a chain of convicting evidence. They would not need to take it to the sheriff. Her father might not want her to do that. It was for him to decide. But if she let Mr. Todman suspect what they had, he would not press a request for Red Wing.

Hastily finishing her work with Dundy and blanketing him crookedly, she saddled a big rawboned roan horse.

As soon as he was warmed up, Kay encouraged him to do his best. Within a short time they were inside Smith's pasture. She found recent traces of hoofs. She followed them, looking eagerly on every side.

Ha! Here the horse had stopped, milling about. Kay dismounted. On the other side of the fence were more tracks. The brush on her side was trampled down. Kay followed the broken line. A plain footprint of a man's shoe. Yes, and here under this brush—what luck! He'd hidden the dead bird. And, yes, his gun! Maybe he had been afraid she would see it. It was not far from here to the highway. He probably had intended to stop for it. But if he had caught a glimpse of Clarke riding Dundy, he might have thought it better to wait until tomorrow. He was an early riser, she knew.

Kay left the gun untouched and carefully replaced the slain bird, minus its tail feathers. Then she started home with a light heart.

It was dark by the time she reached the stables. She called to her mother that she'd come to dinner in a minute. She had to telephone first.

Clarke's mother answered, and she was not at all cordial. No, he was not at home. Mrs. Grant disapproved of girls calling up her son. Kay tried to explain to her that her business with Clarke was important.

His mother answered tartly, "Is there any of your business that you young people do not think is all-important?" And she hung up.

Kay lacked the courage to call her back. She would have to suppress her impatience until morning.

It was less than an hour after sunrise when Clarke's bicycle came rattling up the driveway.

"Hey," he called to Kay, "look what I got!"

"Oh, did the picture turn out?" She ran toward him.

"Take a look." He thrust a cardboard at her.

As plain as could be was Mr. Todman taking aim. And in the picture was the very bush under which he had hidden the bird.

"Only I didn't get the follow-up," mourned Clarke. "I thought I was surely early enough this morning. I cut across the field to that bush you see there in the picture. But the dead bird I'd watched him hide was gone. So I couldn't get a picture of that. He must have caught a glimpse of me—got on his guard anyhow."

Kay pulled a handful of tail feathers out of her pocket. "He didn't find these on his bird, early as he came," she exulted. Quickly she told Clarke her story. "And now it's not too early to call that gentleman and inform him that Red Wing is not available today—or any day. Not till Dad gets back."

While she put through the call, Clarke took a

carrot in to Dundy, then brought him out to brush and rub him, making the best amends he could for his rough treatment of the day before. His whistling slowed as Kay talked on the telephone, then shrilled out with pleased satisfaction as she replaced the receiver.

"He'd missed the tail feathers, all right," said Kay triumphantly. "He wasn't at all anxious for me to talk about a picture I had to show him. In fact it seemed to be quite agreeable to him to stay away from the place entirely. He agreed yes, yes, Red Wing did need a rest. And that is that."

With her heart at rest, Kay brought the mare out of her stall, took off the blanket, and began to groom the lovely coat. Soon she was going to have every horse in the stable in perfect condition. Only happy days were ahead for Red Wing.

Big Tex

PAT FOLINSBEE

CLIMBING to the top rail of the gate to the south field, Jan whistled, a long, low whistle, pitched down and flatted out like the cry of a lake loon. It had been her call for Big Tex ever since she had played with him as a colt and he had come running to nuzzle lumps of sugar from her hand. Now, his head came up inquiringly from his grazing and she repeated the whistle—low and insistent, with a surging optimism.

Big Tex cocked his ears forward as the sound floated away over the prairies. Her grey eyes pleaded as she sent it down to him again. *If only he would respond with his old, joyous whinny and come galloping down the field, his flaming tail adrift on the wind!* But this morning was like all the others that had passed in the month since his accident at Bay Meadows. She knew from the angle of his head that the call meant nothing. It was

139

as though great chunks of his memory had walled off when he fell, plunging him into a world of symbols only half understood.

Pulling a fresh carrot from the back pocket of her faded dungarees, Jan leaped lightly down into the field. Big Tex's eyes were suspicious as she walked slowly up to him and lightly grasped the halter.

"Easy, boy, easy," she murmured soothingly as he jerked his head against her hold. She gave him the carrot and, as he crunched it, she reached out and stroked his muzzle—he had always loved that. When he didn't resist, she let her hand slide gently down his neck and over his burnished shoulder. The hard-packed muscles felt tense and uneasy.

Her eyes traveled on over his tight-knit girth and flanks and back to his smoldering eyes, which reminded her lately of his wild sire, Big Devil— the only horse she had ever feared in the fifteen years since her father had first lifted her to a saddle. She remembered how she had worried that Big Tex might someday grow to be like him. Big Tex, who had been gentle as a kitten since the day he was foaled, and almost human in his dogged affection for her. It seemed incredible that now she had actually to hold him to keep him from flying away. Her wistful recollections were suddenly cut off by her father's whistle from the gate. She turned to answer his wave before she gave Big Tex a final rub and released his halter. His sharp cry and bright, tossing mane breathed defiance as he bounded away to the far corner of the field. Her

140

hands hung helplessly at her sides as she watched his flight, and then she turned and ran toward her father.

"I figured I'd find you out here," John Stevens said. His lean face creased into a grin as he held the gate for her and closed it behind her. "How is he this morning?" He nodded back toward Big Tex.

She sighed and turned up the collar of her leather jacket. "About the same," she said. "Dad, do you think there is any chance that Dr. Alcott will be able to help him?"

"We'll know this morning, Jan. He's the best vet on the prairies. But I wouldn't build on it." He dropped a wiry hand to her shoulder. "Why? Have you figured out something?"

"Well—" Jan flushed, wondering how he always knew when she was leading up to something. "Well, I thought if Doctor Alcott couldn't do any more than the others, then I'd like to take Tex up to the hills. To Andy McDowell's place, it's so isolated and peaceful. The other horses around here seem to keep Tex on edge—they don't give him a chance to find himself."

"Those hills are pretty wild, youngster," he reminded her gently. "I can't leave the ranch right now and I'd hesitate to let you take him alone."

"I know, Dad. But Andy and Jeanne would be there—and I'd be careful. Don't you see—I think it might be really important for Big Tex!"

He rested his forearms along the top rail of the gate, his deep-set eyes focused thoughtfully on the horse.

"Look, Jan," he said finally, "you've got to accept sooner or later that Big Tex may never run again. He's been at the top—he's had his share of glory. For a month now you've worried yourself ragged over him. That isn't any good. It's fine to have faith in your horse, sure—but don't let him break you. He'll do that if you let him."

Jan glanced down, lacing her fingers tightly together. She knew it was her father's indirect way of giving an order. He didn't give them often, but when he did you had to respect them.

"I'm sorry, Dad," she whispered.

"I'm sorry, too, Jan." He turned and tousled her fair, short-cropped hair. "You know I'd give anything to get Big Tex over this—but you're all the family I've got." He smiled the slow smile that meant he was thinking of her mother. Jan could only remember her as being very tall, with a soft voice and shining, auburn hair. Then he glanced at his wrist watch and his voice exploded.

"Holy smokes," he cried. "We'll have to hustle if we want to get to town in time to meet the doctor's train!"

Jan smiled at his apparent alarm, which she knew was contrived to carry them over an awkward moment; and she was still smiling as their eyes met and they turned together back toward the ranch house.

Dr. Alcott didn't fit at all into Jan's preconception. Instead of being tall and rangy like her father, he was short and rotund, with a brusque voice and bushy eyebrows that had the uneasy anchorage of tumbleweeds. Squeezed in between him and her father as they drove back to the ranch she wished suddenly that she had worn one of her neglected summer dresses. Dr. Alcott had a pearl stickpin in his tie.

"Now, John," the elderly doctor said briskly, "tell me more about this horse. Your letter didn't make much sense. What about this fall he took? Was there anything unusual about it?"

"It's hard to say." Her father's resonant voice screened through Jan's swiftly diminishing confidence in the doctor. "The horses were just turning out of the backstretch, in a pack, when suddenly the three lead horses tangled some way and went down. Mel Stott was jockeying Big Tex that day and he said all he could see was hoofs, flying up at him—then they went sailing in. It happened fast."

"Hm-mm." Dr. Alcott drummed his stubby fingers on the dashboard. "And you say he was stunned?"

"Yes, for a couple of days afterward." Jan took comfort from the fact that her father didn't seem to think the doctor's questions were foolish.

"How's he been since you brought him to the ranch?" Dr. Alcott unhinged and carefully wiped his glasses.

"Well. . . ." Mr. Stevens hesitated. "He doesn't even seem to recognize Jan, here, and she practically raised the horse from a colt. Then, when we put him in the main stable with the other horses he went almost crazy—started to kick the side out of his stall—so we put him off in a field by himself."

"How did he like that?" the doctor asked, replacing his glasses and gazing out of the window.

"No real change. He hasn't had any more crazy attacks. But he seems listless, as though the heart had gone out of him. Until you go near him; then he tenses right up."

"Hm-mm." Dr. Alcott's eyebrows contracted. Jan wasn't sure whether at her father's words or at something that had caught his eye out on the prairies. "Your letter mentioned him being sired by a wild stallion," he added, almost as an afterthought.

"That's right." John cramped the wheels in through the gate of the ranch. "A beautiful roan, but wild. The lads captured him up in the hill country, near Andy McDowell's place. We never did get a saddle on him. Texan Susan was the dam. I mentioned bloodlines because I thought it might have some bearing on Tex's trouble."

"It might," the doctor conceded. "That type of cross-breed often produces a high-strung horse; sometimes you get a complete throwback to the dominant strain."

Her father stopped the truck at the ranch house and Jan watched with growing misgivings as the doctor climbed down, fastidiously dusting his coat-tails.

"We thought we might have a bite of breakfast and then take a look at the horse," Mr. Stevens suggested.

144

"Let's look at the horse first," the doctor replied brusquely. "Where do you keep him?"

Mr. Stevens winked at Jan's startled expression and led the way out past the corral.

"Nice layout," the doctor noted as he bounced along. "Good stuff. Well-rooted."

Jan's respect for him rose a notch. He seemed to have a noticing kind of eye.

They waited at the gate while Jan slipped into the field and brought Big Tex back to them.

"Well," the doctor said, "you wouldn't know he was a sick horse to look at him. Fine head."

He removed his gloves and, as Jan steadied Big Tex by the halter, he began a methodical examination. She saw there was nothing fussy about his stubby hands now as they slid expertly over Big Tex's body, feeling, prodding, considering. Big Tex trembled apprehensively and began to paw the turf as the examination stretched into interminable minutes of silence. The doctor's only comment was a faint "hm-mm" as he looked into Tex's eyes. The sick emptiness mushroomed inside her as Dr. Alcott finally straighted up, brushing his hands together.

"There doesn't seem to be anything physically wrong with the horse." He shrugged, obviously puzzled. "Any internal injury would have shown up by now. I suppose you've had all the standard tests taken?"

"Of course. Why do you say nothing *physically* wrong, doctor?" Jan's father asked slowly. Jan's hand tightened on the halter.

"Well, sir. . . ." The doctor took off his glasses again and wiped them meditatively. "It's only opinion, of course. But from what you've told me—and from the tension in the horse while I examined him —I would say he was afraid of something. Like a kid will be afraid of a shadow in the dark until you shine a light and show him it's only a bush or tree."

Jan frowned. She had never known Big Tex to be afraid of anything.

"I also have the feeling," the doctor continued, "that the horse is bottled up. Just waiting to explode. He may be dangerous if that happens. On the other hand, it might be the thing that will snap him back. You have to burst a boil to cure it, you know."

Jan winced at the ugly thought and it set new doubts to churning in her mind.

"Is there any treatment you can suggest?" Her father sounded doubtful, too.

"Nothing much," the doctor said. "I think he should be ridden again. It won't help him to brood around by himself. And if it's possible I'd suggest you get him away from the ranch, away from all contact with other horses for a while."

Jan's breath caught and her excitement triggered as she glanced quickly at her father. He grinned wanly at the obvious plea in her eyes and then rubbed his chin thoughtfully, the way he always did when he was perplexed.

"Jan's anticipated you there, doctor," he admitted finally. "She wanted to take the horse up to Andy McDowell's place."

"Up in the hill country?" Dr. Alcott glanced at her sharply. "Isn't that where they captured his sire?"

"Yes," Mr. Stevens said. "But that was a few years back. Wild herds are scarce now; they were even then. She wouldn't be liable to run into any trouble that way."

"Well, then, it's probably not a bad idea," the doctor said. "To be honest, I wanted you to get him away from your other horses because I'm afraid if he uncorks he may go berserk. That's pure speculation, of course, but you have too many fine horses here to risk it." He pulled on his gloves. "I'd like to go over him again later, but meanwhile, how about that bite of breakfast?"

Jan could hardly breathe for the excitement crowding up in her as she released Big Tex and fell into step with her father. The lines on his face seemed suddenly to have set deeper and some of the swing had gone out of his broad shoulders. But she could tell from the absent-minded way he rumpled her hair as they walked that he was already making up his mind to let her go.

Andy McDowell had built his isolated layout suspended in the hills, partly, he said, because it reminded him of his native Highlands and partly because the meadows were deep and lush up there for the sheep from which he made his livelihood.

"Well, lass," Andy reflected as Jan helped his wife, Jeanne, finish up the breakfast dishes two mornings later. "You quite surprised us—coming up with that horse last night."

"I hope Tex and I won't be a nuisance to you," Jan said.

"Nuisance? Ah, no, quite the contrary, eh, Jeannie?"

Mrs. McDowell smiled her assent. "We always like young company," she said simply.

Andy cleared his throat noisily. "You didn't make too clear what you planned to do with Tex up here, Jan."

"The doctor said just ride him enough to keep him fit." Jan slipped into her leather jacket. "He hopes the quiet will help. It's so beautiful up here."

"Aye." Andy struck a match and held it over his pipe. "It is beautiful—on the surface. But it's still a wilderness underneath." He rose. "Come along; I'll give you a hand with your saddling."

They walked out into the bright sunshine toward the sheep cote where Big Tex was quartered. The hills looked scrubbed and freshly green after a night's rain and the air had a clean lift to it that left a burning in Jan's chest.

Big Tex whinnied restlessly as they entered his improvised stall. Jan had been up at dawn to tend to his feeding and watering and her heart skipped as she noticed that not a grain of oats remained. He had only nibbled his food at the ranch.

"He's a handsome big beast all right," Andy said admiringly as Jan lifted her light racing saddle and bridle from the wall. "But he's a wild one—you can see it there in his eyes."

148

"He was sired by that wild roan stallion they captured up here a few years back. You must remember him, Andy?"

"Aye, I do. He was more tiger than horse, that one. So this is his son?" Andy helped her adjust the saddle girth. "I don't see how you sit such a saddle," he marveled. "Looks no more sturdy than an oatcake."

Jan laughed. "Do you ever see any wild horses around, Andy?" she said as she bridled Big Tex. He resisted the bit a moment before he took it, etching a corner of worry in her mind. He had never resisted before.

"Not often, now." Andy stepped back as she led Big Tex from the stall. "I see hoofprints now and again—but the horses are shy as quicksilver."

Jan patted Big Tex on the neck and swung lightly up into the saddle. His feet were dancing nervously against the springy, damp turf. He seemed keyed-up. Jan had never known him to be so taut— with uneasy shivers going through him.

"Easy, boy, easy," she soothed him.

"He's skittish, lass," Andy said. "You better not take the hill trails. They're rough and confusing. Take him over by the salt meadows; the grass is good and there's level spots where you can run him."

"That's the trail over the hogsback, isn't it?" Jan said.

"Aye," Andy said. "You'll be back for lunch?"

"Long before," she assured him. "I want him to take it easy today. He's all knotted up."

149

"I can see that. Well, he's in good care."

The damp scent of upland pines stirred restlessly as Jan and Big Tex took the rise of the hogsback. The wide sweep of the sky and the silver clarity of the morning washed away Jan's early apprehension about Big Tex's reaction to this strange country. He seemed alert and eager now, straining forward as though he recognized the freedom of the vast expanse of the hills.

At the crest the trail divided, with a left branch leading down through the thinning pines to the salt meadows, and a narrow, right branch continuing along the crest and disappearing into the thickly wooded contours of the succeeding hill. Jan had no memory of that trail; it seemed new and freshly broken. She must remember to ask Andy about it when she got back.

She neck-reined Big Tex lightly to indicate the left fork. His head came up sharply at her touch. Then he snorted and balked, digging his front hoofs stubbornly into the turf. Jan took a firmer grip on the reins as she scanned the left trail for any cause. But there was nothing.

"Come on, boy," she urged him gently. "What is it, Tex? Come on, now, go down." She reached down and patted his shoulder. It felt like stone.

Suddenly he snorted again in protest, half reared and turned down the right branch of the fork. Jan pulled him short and he tossed his head violently, trying to shake off the hold of the bit. Suppressing the uneasiness in her mind, Jan turned him back with infinite patience. He responded resentfully, his

150

ears flattened back. And then, as she tried to turn him into the left fork, he refused again.

Jan eased her hold on the reins and talked to him softly, stroking his neck, with slow, soothing gestures.

"What is it, Tex?" she said softly. "What are you afraid of? Do you want to take the right fork, Tex? Is that it, boy?"

He whinnied softly. Jan sat back in her saddle, trying to puzzle it out. Big Tex had always obeyed eagerly, but now he was behaving like a stubborn, badly schooled horse.

She frowned and, after another moment of disturbed consideration, decided to give in to him. The doctor had advised her not to force him.

"All right, Tex," she murmured. "Away you go." A short investigation of the trail might satisfy his curiosity.

He wheeled sharply and started off down the trail at a trot. Jan had to hold him from breaking into a canter. The path wound torturously in a series of steep switchbacks that swung upward along the shoulder of the hill succeeding the hogsback. Big Tex never wavered in his sure-footed ascent. Once, where the thick underbrush gave way to a lip-shaped opening, Jan tried to turn him back, but his head went down and he plunged stubbornly on.

Suddenly they looped over the shoulder, a razorlike edge against the backdrop of the sky. The hillside dropped away before then in terraced ledges, leading down to a natural amphitheatre cradled in the hills. A chill gripped her as Big Tex stopped short and her eye dropped swiftly down the slopes. There, far below them, a small band of wild horses grazed peacefully on the valley floor.

She knew instantly it had been no whim of Big Tex's that had led him down the right fork. Of course! This herd had been using the baffling trail as a traverse to the salt meadows, probably moving by night from their hidden retreat. And Big Tex had known it on the hogsback or perhaps even earlier—sound and scent carried far on the night air.

Jan dismounted hastily, heeping a tight hold on the reins. Big Tex stamped impatiently, his ears pitched forward, as she ran her hand over his shoulder. The guard hairs were erect, bristling and electric to the touch. Suddenly a wild cry curdled from his lips and he reared, fighting fiercely to break her hold.

She jerked him back, alarm knotting in her throat. *She had to get him away!*

His hoofs jabbed savagely into the turf and the half-mad scream again froze in the still air.

"Easy, boy, easy!" Jan cried, trying with all her strength to turn his head and lead him back down the trail. He reared again and, in the surging force of it, she almost lost him. Desperately she sawed the bit against his mouth and, twisting the reins around her wrists, yanked him down. Using the bit as gently as she could, she forced him to follow back into the screen of pines along the ridge.

She talked to him softly, urgently, never ceasing

the soothing patter of her words. When they were concealed, she turned to him to rub his muzzle, hoping that familiar gesture would calm him. And then she saw his eyes! Hate, rage and uncontrolled excitement flamed in their black depths. *They were Big Devil's eyes!* The realization drained the color from her face and choked off the flow of words in her throat.

Big Tex trumpeted again to be free. His wild blood had finally erupted, flooding out all recognition of her as anything but an enemy dictating obedience with a cruel steel bit. *What was it Dr. Alcott had said? Someday he might explode!* And now he was fighting her—seeing these hills as sanctuary from the bewildering cadence of hoofs flying back at him, ready to strike with blinding force, and from falling, twisting bodies.

In that instant she understood Tex's struggle to be free. The thin steel bit was the last remnant of the frail veneer they had imposed over his wild spirit. It had begun to crack with his fall and now, recognizing his own, it had sheered completely away.

Sometimes they throw back to the dominant strain! She remembered how she had only half-listened to those words.

Doubt and dismay struggled within her. If she released Big Tex he would rush down there—perhaps to his death. Certainly he would have to fight for acceptance. And yet if she held him back she knew she would break his spirit completely—for-

ever. What was it the doctor had said? *A boil has
to burst to be cured!*

She tried to reason it out, but there was no time.
It was too late; holding him back now she would
only selfishly destroy him. It had to be the other
way.

Slowly she wound up the reins on her wrist and
held him short. She couldn't look up at him as she
reached and unfastened the saddle girth. The tiny
saddle and blanket fell almost noiselessly to the
ground. He seemed to understand her movements,
for he held steady as she reached up and slipped
the bridle down over his ears, and gently pulled the
bit away from his mouth.

He was free. For a split instant he stood, towering magnificently above her, and then his head
tossed up and back, and his mane and tail streamed
fire as he wheeled and streaked down into the valley.

Jan stopped and picked up the saddle and blanket. She wanted to cry. But there were no tears.
She threw the saddle over her shoulder and half
turned down the trail back to the hogsback. Just
then a stallion's trumpeting challenge froze her step.
An answering note trumpeted back. *That would be
Big Tex!* There was triumph in that second voice.

She let the saddle slip to the ground. She couldn't
watch. Yet something stronger than her will drew
her back through the trees and out to the edge of
the valley, the bridle still trailing aimlessly from her
hand.

Big Tex stood his ground at one end of the tiny

amphitheatre. His head was up and proud—like a king, Jan thought; his superb body glittered in the sunlight. At the other end a half dozen mares huddled together and advancing from them was a rough-coated chestnut stallion, not quite as tall as Big Tex, but stocky, thick through the chest, with heavy shoulders and muscular hindquarters tapering down into powerful legs and rock-sharpened hoofs.

Jan's breathing stilled as the space between the two diminished. The challenge again ricocheted between them. Jan saw Big Tex hesitate, half turn away.

"Hold your ground, Tex!" she whispered fiercely. "Don't let him think you're afraid!"

The two stallions circled warily and then, with an unearthly scream, the chestnut closed the gap, his hoofs flying. They met, rearing back with their fore-hoofs slashing out blindly. As their bodies came thundering down, their bared teeth tore for each other's throats. Big Tex's tail swept angrily across his back and a dull, rasping roar rose in his throat as the chestnut stallion circled. Big Tex planted his front legs wide and firm and his head was down so that his forelock brushed the grass as he steeled himself for the next impact.

The chestnut closed fast, head-on; then, with the cunning of the wilds, hurled himself suddenly broadside and plunged down, catching Tex off-guard. Lunging forward and heaving his back in a bowed arch he caught Big Tex beneath the flank and threw him violently to the rock-strewn ground, his legs flailing helplessly.

Jan sucked her breath as Big Tex thudded into the turf and the chestnut reared above him to crash his hoofs into Big Tex's chest. But the terror in her throat choked off as Big Tex half-rolled, half-threw himself to take the deadly hoofs in a glancing blow down off his shoulder. Then he was up.

Almost unaware of her movements Jan crept, inch by inch, down the rough side of the valley until she was standing on the last ledge above them. Her eyes never once strayed from Big Tex as again and again he evaded and baffled the on-rushing, foam-flecked stallion. After the first raging struggle and fall, the two horses measured each rush carefully. They seemed to recognize that neither was an easy foe to be whipped in one vain-glorious charge.

Standing helplessly on the ledge, Jan shuddered, knowing the battle was approaching a climax. The trumpeting roar of the horses had hushed as their blood-smeared, sweating bodies maneuvered warily in the bright sunlight.

Suddenly it came. With an ominous note sounding low in his throat, Big Tex swung unpredictably to the offensive. His long body seemed to explode upward like a flame and he sheered his forelegs savagely across the front of his body, catching the chestnut stallion half-balanced as he reared back to meet the assault. Raked clean by the shattering, unexpected blow, the wild stallion faltered. His supporting hind legs gave way in the soft turf and he somersaulted backward. Instantly Big Tex leaped astride the chestnut's fallen body, pinning him down. Then with an ugly roar he upreared his steel-shod hoofs in the final, menacing gesture.

Jan gritted her teeth and closed her eyes tight in horror. In the same instant she heard the torn cry breaking from the pinioned stallion. It was a lost cry, rising above the stillness, clear and beautiful.

She looked up again to see Big Tex, his magnificent, upreared body hovering uncertainly, then half-twisting into a fall, down and away from the body of the chestnut. And he stood, his flanks heaving.

The fight was over. The chestnut rose haltingly and, without a glance at Big Tex, turned, with the age-old humility of defeat, to take an inconspicuous place among the bleating, huddled mares. His behavior seemed to conform to some immutable design, patterned and stamped out through the centuries that wild horses had roamed the hills.

Big Tex made no move to follow. His proud eyes surveyed the herd amost disdainfully and his silken tail swayed back and forth like an uncertain banner. In his triumph he seemed suddenly awkward and ill at ease. His hoofs danced and his nostrils flared questioningly toward the other horses. Finally he cantered over to where they awaited his command and stopped short, dissatisfied.

Jan wanted to cry out to him, but something strangled her voice. Her hands doubled into tight fists as Big Tex tossed his head and thundered his displeasure at the herd, scattering the advances of the mares.

Then, without volition, her lips pursed together. The whistle came faintly at first and then floated out over the valley.

A strange calm washed through her as Big Tex wheeled, a startled whinny breaking in his throat. She drew herself up to her full height. Again she sent her call down to him, clear and unbroken in the silence. This time she waved.

Big Tex's eye caught the movement and he broke toward her with a sharp, joyful cry. Eternity seemed spun into that second to Jan. And then he was there, whimpering softly. She slipped her arm up around his blood-streaked neck and pressed her cheek tearfully against his soft, quivering muzzle.

When her heart stopped pounding, she stooped and picked up the fallen bridle. Gently she slipped it over his ears and offered him the bit. He took it without resistance, cocking his ears back and forth expectantly as she gave his muzzle a rewarding rub.

Grasping the reins lightly, she led him up to the rim of the valley. There she stopped to look back. The tiny valley was deserted—the wild horses had vanished. She had not even been aware of their going—like quick-silver, Andy had said.

She noticed that the sun was at its zenith. They would have to hurry. But something stayed her hand on the reins as she glanced up at Big Tex's immobile, sculptured head. His eyes were glowing and magnificent sparks burned in their depths. But not for her. His gaze was traveling far out, over the hills. His nostrils flared wide and the wind rustled in his flame-colored mane as a low whinny broke from his throat and echoed, lonely and sad, down and across the walls of the valley. Her heart closed tight as the sound trembled and whispered away. Then Big Tex's head came down and nuzzled gently against her shoulder, turning her down the long trail to the salt meadows and home.

Black Satin

JACK HANKINS

EVELYN strode up to the rustic sign, stood behind it. The sign read "Red Thorn Ranch," in red-gold letters. But that didn't interest her. What was going on in the corral did: Florence was going to ride Black Satin, the Satin, the little mare Evelyn had raised. Like everything else, it belonged to the estate, was owned by Florence and her husband John Friar. Yet in her heart Evelyn felt that Satin was hers. She had hand-raised the little mare from a puny colt, had broken her to the bridle and the saddle, had been the only one to ride her.

Evelyn watched Tom Linsey lead Satin to the corral gate, saw him give the reins to Florence.

Quickly Florence thrust her foot in the saddle, mounted. Satin gave a quick lunge, but Florence pulled her up, held her taut. Then Florence slacked rein a trifle, and Satin danced forward.

Later, Evelyn saw Satin come galloping in from the meadow. Florence rode easily. She was a good rider. But she demanded much of her mounts.

Evelyn had heard Old Tom muttering about her riding her horses to death.

"Hand me my riding whip, Evelyn," Florence ordered.

Startled, Evelyn quickly grabbed the whip from the corral. Florence grasped it, headed Satin for the pole fence that formed part of her park near the big house.

But, as Satin approached the fence, she set her feet, slid to a stop. Florence came down with the whip, but Satin dodged, refused the jump.

Florence rode slowly back. Color was deep in her cheeks.

"She's never jumped before," Evelyn said.

"She'll jump for me," Florence retorted.

After a moment's rest, Florence again set her at the fence. As she approached it, Florence jabbed her with her spurs, came down with the whip. Satin lurched wildly with fright, but Florence held her to the fence.

Satin began the jump. But she was running too fast, and the bit was too strong in her tender mouth. She couldn't gather. Florence stood up in the stirrups, gave her her head. But too late. She lurched, hit the poles with a crash, and both went down.

Evelyn ran toward them. Tom Linsey came running. When Evelyn reached them, Florence, who had been thrown on the grass beyond the fence, was getting to her feet. Satin lay crumpled in the broken poles, struggling feebly, beating her head on the ground trying to rise. One back leg was caught in the poles, twisted in an unnatural position.

The foreman rushed up to Florence.

"Are you hurt?" he inquired anxiously.

"I'm all right," Florence replied. "You'd better see to the horse."

Tom turned to the horse. Evelyn was kneeling by Satin, talking to her, stroking her neck. The little mare was struggling, trying to rise. Her eyes looked wild, frightened.

"Get up, Satin," Evelyn said, urging her, pulling at the reins.

But the little mare flopped her head, couldn't get her legs under her.

"Is she badly hurt?" Florence asked.

Tom shook his head. "I'm afraid so," he muttered, looking down at the black mare. "She hasn't been jumped before. This fence is pretty high."

"But she refused it when I first put her to it," Florence answered. "You know when you let a horse refuse and let her get away with it, you may ruin her as a jumper. I realize now that this fence was too high to begin with. She's so small."

Tom frowned, finally unlaced the saddle, pulled the lacings from under Satin. "Try her again, Evelyn," he said.

Evelyn stopped stroking her and talking to her, took the reins and pulled, coaxed her. Satin struggled, finally fell back panting.

Tom shook his head. "No use."

Florence looked at her with a set face, then

turned toward the big house. "Destroy her," she said crisply.

"Oh, no," Evelyn cried, looking after Florence. She had never hated anyone as she hated Florence at that moment.

Tom looked grim. "It's really the kindest thing to do—put her out of her misery. She's bad hurt. If I called a vet, he'd probably tell me the same thing."

"You just can't do that," Evelyn cried wildly. "Let me take care of her. I raised her from a colt. I can make her well. Oh, please!"

After more pleading, Tom at last agreed to let her try. He summoned a hired man with a hay sled and team. The three loaded Satin on the sled, and the team pulled her to an old feed shed behind the blacksmith shop and machinery house. There, they unloaded her, put her on her feet near the wall of the shed, so that she would have some support.

"Don't let anyone know the mare's here," Tom warned her somberly. "If Florence finds out I've disobeyed her, it might cost me my job."

Evelyn stood by Satin, stroked her, spoke soothingly to her. The little mare trembled, held up one leg.

Evelyn brought a sack of oats and a sack of hay. From the gardener's cottage where she and her father lived she took an apple. Though she held the food to Satin's mouth, the horse would not take a bite. She brought a bucket of water, but the little mare would not drink. She just stood as though dazed, her eyes dulled.

That evening Evelyn told her father of the horse and also of her determination to sleep in the shed with Satin.

"I'd hate to get in bad with the boss's wife," he replied, frowning. But, when she assured him she would be careful, he helped her carry a camp bed to the shed.

With a heavy heart, Evelyn lay down beside the little mare. She listened to her breathing, heard each move she made during the night. But, in the morning, she still lived, apparently without any change in her condition. Evelyn again tried to get her to eat. She even pushed the apple into her mouth. But the horse wouldn't chew it. And again she refused water.

That night again Evelyn slept on the camp bed beside the mare. Listening to her breathing, she had a difficult time going to sleep. Finally she did sleep but woke with a start. The dawn was gray. Satin was moving. Evelyn got up, stroked her neck, then lifted the water pail to her.

The little mare stuck her muzzle into the pail, began to drink. In delight Evelyn held the bucket until it was empty. Then she gave her the apple. She held oats up to her, but this Satin refused. Evelyn ran, drew another pail of water. She held it until Satin had emptied it.

For the next few days Satin's appetite continued to improve. Within ten days it was normal. Yet she scarcely moved from the place in the shed. Finally Evelyn took her mane and led her the few feet to the other side of the shed. She moved awkwardly, with a grotesque stride. She wouldn't walk without being led. She held the one back leg up.

Evelyn waited until she saw Florence drive off in the station wagon, then led Satin out and tied her to the fence. Each day she would watch for Florence to leave, then would walk Satin around in the warm sun.

Each day Satin's stride improved with the gentle exercise in the sun. When she seemed almost normal, Evelyn mounted her, petted her much, rode her slowly and for only a few minutes each day until she became accustomed to a rider. Though she seemed frightened the first time the girl mounted, she soon became as accustomed to Evelyn on her back as she was before her accident. And the old gloss and sheen that had given her the name Black Satin returned to her coat, and the brightness returned to her eyes.

Evelyn extended the riding sessions each time Florence was away from the ranch. She galloped down into the meadow, through the park. And she commenced to teach Satin to jump, beginning with obstacles no more than a foot high and easily breakable to the touch of a hoof and gradually essayed higher barriers. Satin seemed to enjoy each higher jump as though a test of her strength. And her stride was what it was before the accident, the ever-eager, sparkling pace.

Then one day Evelyn galloped in from the mead-

166

ow and was stopped in the barnyard by Tom Linsey, the foreman. "Put Satin in the corral with the other horses—and quick," he ordered. "Florence came back when you were down in the meadow. She's been inspecting things and has found the shed. She can see a horse has been kept there. She's suspicious."

"What did you tell her?" Evelyn queried, tumbling off the mare and hurrying her into the corral.

"Told her we had a sick horse in the shed a long while ago," Tom mumbled. "Don't think she believed the 'long time ago' part anyway. Started asking a lot of questions. Now hurry."

Evelyn stood by the corral gate with her fingers crossed. Florence and Tom at last reached the corral, climbed up the poles, perched on top.

"A new horse?" Florence inquired with the suddenness that nearly made Evelyn's heart stop beating. "The little black mare."

Tom looked worried, mumbled something.

"She's pretty," Florence continued. "She'd be a good entry in the Denton Horseshow and Auction. I want to save the bigger animals for hunters and jumpers, and still I wanted an entry that would uphold the tradition of the ranch. She'll be our entry."

Tom agreed enthusiastically, but Evelyn's heart fell. Satin would surely be bought. She was going to lose her after she had raised her, after she had nursed her back to health. Satin was far dearer now to her than she had ever been before the accident.

"You know, there's something familiar about the mare," Florence murmured. She looked directly down at Evelyn.

Evelyn felt like sinking in her boots. The foreman coughed loudly, muttered, "You probably saw her mother," and suggested that they walk over to see the new trees that had been set out in the park.

Florence's mouth seemed firm and set as she climbed down from the fence and strode toward the park, followed by the foreman.

Did Florence recognize Satin?

The horseshow was only a week away, and Satin was ordered to be groomed. Though it was the stable boy's job, Evelyn took over.

Florence was reasonable in most things, but she insisted that her orders be carried out instantly. Many a man on the ranch had been fired for even delaying. And if she knew about Satin, that her orders to destroy the horse had been ignored—she might sell Satin on purpose.

With a set and white face, Evelyn went about getting Black Satin ready for the show and the sale. Early each morning she rode her into the meadow, put her through her jumps. She curried her until her coat shone like the material for which she was named.

The day that Satin was to be taken to the show Evelyn was at the stable at dawn. She saddled the little mare and raced her down into the meadow. Never had she seemed so eager. Evelyn rode her with the wildness of despair. Satin seemed to feel her mood and to join in it. She went over the jumps as though she were winged. She seemed never to tire.

At last Evelyn turned her toward the stable. She raced madly. The morning was crisp and cold. She was flying through the air instead of riding.

Nearing the stable, Evelyn, in a moment of wildness, turned the little mare toward the fence, the fence on which she had nearly killed herself when Florence set her to it. Evelyn had never tried her on this jump. It had been built higher when it had been mended after the accident.

As she approached the fence, Evelyn started to pull her in. But the little mare, filled with the zest of the gambol and the morning, took the bit in her mouth and hurtled toward the jump. Evelyn jerked on the reins, but Satin sailed on. She didn't dare try again for fear of throwing her off her stride, and crashing her into the poles.

She raised herself in her stirrups. Satin gathered for the leap. The little mare's hooves left the turf.

The mare seemed to float through the air with her legs tucked in. She was on top of the poles. Standing in the stirrups, leaning forward, Evelyn slacked rein. Satin's front feet struck the turf of the park. She had made it! She was running on the other side of the barrier.

Evelyn pulled her up. Both she and the horse were panting. And she was glowing inside. Satin had performed magnificently.

"Bravo!" came a voice near her. "Wonderful!"

Evelyn whirled. Florence was walking toward her. "You and Satin seem to get along pretty well," Florence said, putting a hand on the mare's neck.

Satin? Then she knew, Evelyn thought. "Oh, yes, I know this is Satin," Florence continued, rubbing the black, glossy neck. "I may be mistaken about a good many things but not about a horse. I recognized her in the corral."

"Oh, I just couldn't let her be destroyed," Evelyn cried. "I disobeyed you, but I just had to save her."

Evelyn braced herself for the expected explosion, but strangely, it didn't come. Florence didn't even look angry!

"I'm happy for once I was disobeyed," Florence said softly. "I've felt badly ever since the accident. It was my fault for putting this little, untrained mare to that jump. I could hardly restrain my happiness when I saw her the other day alive and well."

"She'll make someone a nice mount," Evelyn remarked, thinking of the horse show and auction.

"Why not for you?" Florence asked.

Evelyn's mouth opened in astonishment.

"Yes, she's yours," Florence said. "I won't break up the team. I love horses and horsemanship. Every morning for the last week I've been up early to watch you and Satin. I guess you were too absorbed to notice a woman with a pair of field glasses standing in the park."

Evelyn could only gasp her thanks. She had hoped

170

that Satin would remain on the ranch. But owning her was beyond her fondest dreams.

"I would be pleased if you would ride her in the show," Florence added, "under the ranch's colors. I'll select one of my hunters for the auction—and hope no one will bid on him."

Florence turned toward the house, and Evelyn started Satin toward the stables. She was still breathless. But she was determined: Black Satin would be the slickest, glossiest mount ever to enter the Denton Horseshow.

They would leave in two hours for Denton! Well, it was time enough to curry Satin and polish her harness.

Evelyn thought that she and Florence could be good friends. They both loved horses and admired Black Satin.

Tall as the Stars

◆━◆━◆━◆━◆

JANET LAMBERT

THE small Army post was lazy in the warm fall sunshine. The parade ground, with its surrounding circle of houses, was empty as Judy Roderick scuffled through the dried, rustling leaves on her lawn, tying a limp red ribbon to a stubby yellow pigtail. As she reached her own porch, she gave her hair a last yank—and looked up to see her sister Cynthia looking at her with disapproval.

Cynthia's curls floated loosely on her shoulders, and her eyes, instead of being wide apart and candidly blue, like Judy's, were violets hidden in a deep hedge of lashes. A junior in high school, she was always so intent on her own crowd that she rarely noticed the freshman who was her sister.

Today, however, she put out a hand to stop Judy. "Are you riding in the show tonight?" she asked.

"Sure. Aren't you?"

"I don't know." Her sister's tone was sad, and

173

Judy's eyes opened wide. "I have a terrible problem," Cynthia went on. "Sit down for a minute, will you?"

It was not unusual for Judy to be on the receiving end of a problem, but as it always meant lending Cynthia something, the younger girl was wary. "What's wrong?" she asked. "Charlemagne all right?"

"I suppose so. He's such a stupid goat I don't really care."

"He's a wonderful horse! Dad says—"

"I don't care what Dad says. I'll never get him around the course tonight. I wish I were as good a rider as you are."

Something hammered a warning inside Judy's breast. "You ride fine," she countered quickly. "I bet Charlemagne will win the class."

"He would if *you* rode him. Would you—and let me ride Jack Snipe?"

"No!" Judy flung back her head. "Listen," she said. "You got Charlemagne, when Dad bought us each a horse, because you cried and said you were older. He's lots better than Jack Snipe—or he could be—and you know it. But I've worked hard on Jack, while you just get dressed up and walk along the bridle paths with a lot of boys. If your horse can't win a class it's your fault."

She tried to rise, but Cynthia pulled her back. "Wait a minute!" she wailed. "You don't know how important it is for me to win tonight. If you won't let me ride Jack Snipe—"

"You can just bet I won't!"

174

"Listen a minute, Judy. You know how I hate history, and how poor my marks have been. This afternoon Mr. MacClendon bawled me out in front of the whole class. He's awfully sarcastic—and when he asked if there was *anything* I was good at, I flared up and said—"

"That you could jump in horse shows," finished Judy.

"Yes. And he looked so amazed that I—well, I guess I laid it on pretty thick, because when I finished telling about the shows and things here at Fort Arden, he said he thought he'd come out to the show tonight!"

"Well, you'll have to make good then," declared Judy.

"I can't—not on Charlemagne! But I know I could win with Jack Snipe."

"Because I've trained him! No. He's my horse and I'm riding him."

Cynthia burst into tears. "I think you're just selfish and mean," she sobbed. "You know Mr. MacClendon will shame me before the whole class."

Judy knew what a build-up Cynthia must have given the horse show—the jumps and the flags, the Army band with its stirring marches. How she must have described the excitement of the general's entrance. And then, because she knew all civilians are interested in the strange world of an Army post, she would have launched into a day at Fort Arden, to lead Mr. MacClendon away from the point of his lecture.

Judy knew how clear the notes of reveille

sounded, floating across the early morning air; with what precision the soldiers drilled on the parade ground, marching proudly past under the watchful folds of Old Glory. She loved the sunset gun that stopped the girls and boys on bicycles, the roller skaters, the people in their cars, and held them at attention while the great flag slid slowly down into waiting arms. She loved it all, especially the peaceful sound of taps proclaiming that all was well. And she felt sure that Mr. MacClendon would want to come out to the post to see for himself.

A whistle from a house a short distance away jerked her back to the present, and she turned to see a boy loping across the intervening lawns.

Cynthia dabbed hurriedly at her tears. "I'll just die if you shame me before—"

"Before Bill Hearndon," said Judy grimly. "I get it now. You really want to show off for Bill—not your history teacher."

"Well, sort of. I think he's going to ask me to the Halloween dance. He's wonderful!"

Judy, too, thought Bill was wonderful. He had moved to the post a month ago, and she had discovered how nice he was while she helped him build a pen around his doghouse. Although an upperclassman, Bill never failed to say "Hi, Judy," on the school bus, and sometimes he would stop and talk with her about Jack Snipe.

She had had three whole weeks of enjoying Bill —and now, Cynthia wanted him. Just as she had wanted Judy's best sweater and her gold bracelet, now she wanted Bill Hearndon and Jack Snipe. A depressing wave of futility swept over Judy. When had it ever done her any good to fight against Cynthia?

"Please," Cynthia was whispering. "Oh, please, Judy!"

Judy sighed. After all, a senior wouldn't want to tag around with a freshman forever—not when he could be with Cynthia. So as Bill came up the porch steps she said, "Oh, all right. Do you want to practice now?"

"Of course not, darling!" Cynthia smiled at Bill. "We're going over to the P.X."

"Want to come along, Jude?" Bill's grin was inviting, but Judy shook her head.

"No, thanks. Guess I'd better see about my tack for tonight."

She watched them cross the parade ground, and then she cut across the tennis courts to the stables. Jack Snipe leaned over the door of his box stall. He was just a brown horse, wellbred, with a long, slender neck and intelligent face. As she laid her cheek against his velvet nose, she reached out to pat Charlemagne. He was so beautiful it made one gasp. His registration papers called him a chestnut, but his coat was shining gold, and he had a small white blaze on his forehead, and four dancing white feet.

"Cynthia could have made you a wonder horse," she said as she gave them each a handful of oats.

Then she hunted up a groom. "Please put my saddle on Charlemagne tonight," she told him. "I'm going to ride him."

177

"Miss Judy!" Private Jones dropped his can of saddle soap. "You've been working so hard with Jack Snipe for that teen-agers' class! What's happened? Don't you want to win?"

"Not so very much." She couldn't tell him that she had wanted Bill to see her win with Jack Snipe, nor that Cynthia wanted to ride for him, too. So she only said, "Cynthia's going to ride Jack Snipe tonight. I think she can handle him."

She walked slowly home, and as slowly put on her riding clothes. I didn't have to do it, she thought, as she tied her fractious hair into a pony's tail on the back of her neck. Dad would have backed me up.

Judy had always been his favorite. Ever since she was a toddler, following him along the picket line, inspecting the horses and prescribing for their injuries, he had called her Corporal. And as she grew older, his interest in horses had been hers. She had led the horses in and out of their stalls, watering, cleaning, polishing bits and stirrups.

But at dinner that night Colonel Roderick seemed satisfied to accept the change of horses, and listened as Cynthia chattered. Her small chin was pointed above a white stock, and her curls were caught into a net and would make a neat roll under a smart black derby. Judy ate her dinner silently.

But when they were on the way to the riding hall she said earnestly, "Listen, Cee. You think Jack Snipe's a cinch to ride, but he isn't. He can run out

178

like a flash just before a jump, when you can't do a thing."

"I know how to ride," Cynthia laughed. "Just keep your mind on Charlemagne."

The riding hall was already beginning to fill and the tanbark-covered arena was ablaze with lights. Officers and their wives were finding seats in the grandstand at one end, while in an improvised paddock at the other, grooms walked the horses in a circle.

Judy walked through the tanbark, studying the jumps, figuring how Jack Snipe—not Charlemagne —could weave his way among them.

"You dope," she scolded herself. "You shouldn't want him to win."

As she crawled through the bars of the paddock fence, Cynthia joined her. Jones checked her stirrups and the saddle girth and she began to move Charlemagne around in a circle. She saw that Jack Snipe regarded Cynthia doubtfully, and danced a little when she tried to mount him.

At last the general arrived and the show began. "Teen-agers' class," the announcer said through the public-address system. "Eight jumps. Time will be counted in the jump-off in case of a tie. First rider—Richard Compton."

When "Cynthia Roderick" was called, Judy prayed softly, "Please, Jack Snipe, take them all clean, for me."

But Jack Snipe was nervous. He had difficulty in lifting himself over the first jump; the second was

179

a double oxer, and he stared at it as if he had never seen one before. But he managed it, and the rest of the jumps, in an awkward performance, straining to free his head.

"You choked him up," Judy scolded when Cynthia rode in. "You'll never win the jump-off that way."

Her turn was next. Charlemagne was reluctant to exert himself, and she pricked him with her spurs, before she turned him toward the first jump. "Sorry, old fellow," she said. "Steady, now. You can do it."

He took the jump cleanly, and tried so hard on the others that Judy forgot she didn't care about winning, and found herself coaxing, talking, and loving the way his ears came back to listen. He sailed over the last jump with beautiful grace.

"Congratulations!" Bill was hanging over the wall of the paddock, talking to Cynthia. "Swell going," he went on, grasping her hand. "I'm pulling for you to win."

"Me?" Judy asked. "Why?"

"Because you took a bum horse and gave a whale of a good ride. What made you do it, Judy? Let Cynthia have your horse, I mean?"

"I wanted to."

"Then see it through—and win."

But she turned away from him. "I'll wait to decide," she told herself.

Finally four riders were left to compete in the jump-off: Si Craig, Marty Johnson, Cynthia, and herself. She sighed as she looked at Cynthia on Jack Snipe. If he won, she could be happy; if he lost, it was no good winning without him.

The starter dropped his red flag and Marty Johnson swung out on the course. His time was good, but Si's was better. Judy, walking Charlemagne in a circle to keep him calm, watched the gate open for Cynthia. Jack Snipe went out like a breeze. He sailed over the jumps. Across the hall, and over. Turn. Over. His head was free, and he forgot that Cynthia was crouched over his neck.

"She's not using a bearing rein," Judy muttered as Jack Snipe thundered along the wall of the riding hall. "She'll have to hold him in." Then she shouted, "Hold him in to the jump, Cynthia!" for Jack Snipe had decided he'd had enough. He shot to the left, by-passed the rails and then whirled around. Cynthia almost went off, but managed to cling ungracefully around his neck, while the gallery applauded.

Then it was Judy's turn. Jack Snipe had lost—should Charlemagne try to win? Loyalty to her own horse, eagerness for Bill's admiration, vied with each other.

Charlemagne took the first jumps easily, and suddenly her decision was made. "I must do what is best for him," she thought. "I must be fair to him." So she helped him at the jumps with encouraging, loving talk, and let him round his turns without pushing him. It was a good ride, but the pleasure was ruined by the black cloud on Cynthia's face when they returned to the paddock.

"I suppose you thought it was funny," she stormed, "to let me ride a quitter."

"He isn't a quitter," Judy hotly defended Jack Snipe. "I warned you to hold him in."

When the announcer called the time that gave her second place, she turned Charlemagne into the ring behind Si. Marty fell in third, and Cynthia brought up the rear. She knew how Cynthia would hate the white fourth-place ribbon she had won.

But Charlemagne arched his neck, when the general's wife hooked the red ribbon on his bridle, as proudly as if it had been the winner's blue. He cantered happily back to the paddock and butted his head against Jones' chest.

"Sure was a pretty ride, Miss Judy," Jones praised.

"Thank you, Jones," she answered. "He's a sweet horse." She swung her leg over the saddle, then stared down in surprise at Bill.

"Jump!" he ordered. "Let's get some fresh air before we see the rest of the show."

Judy slid down, and let Bill keep her hand as they walked outside.

"There'll be a lot more shows this winter," Bill said. "How about working our horses together, then battling each other for a blue?"

He grinned at her companionably and Judy smiled back. "I'd love to, Bill," she answered a little breathlessly, because her heart was pounding in an odd, but happy, way.

The sweet notes of Tattoo floated from a bugle

182

on the parade ground. The night air was cool and soft, and Judy looked up at the sky's bright stars. She need only stand on tiptoe to reach up and touch them, she thought.